"Who in blazes are you?" the dead guy asked. "And what are you doing?"

"You were dead!" Zoë exclaimed breathlessly from where she lay under him. "Look at you! You're covered in blood! I was only trying to help."

He blinked.

She frowned. "I was about to give you mouth-to-mouth."

He blinked again. Then the corner of his lips curved up. If she didn't know better, she'd say they curved up naughtily.

"Okay," he said. Two seconds later he'd spun them so she was on top of him again. He lifted his chin and closed his eyes. "Go for it."

Dear Reader,

June brings you four high-octane reads from Silhouette Romantic Suspense, just in time for summer. Steaming up your sunglasses is Nina Bruhns's hot romance, *Killer Temptation* (#1516), which is the first of a thrilling new trilogy, SEDUCTION SUMMER. In this series, a serial killer is murdering amorous couples on the beach and no lover is safe. You won't want to miss this sexy roller coaster ride! Stay tuned in July and August for Sheri WhiteFeather's and Cindy Dees's heart-thumping contributions, *Killer Passion* and *Killer Affair*.

USA TODAY bestselling author Marie Ferrarella enthralls readers with *Protecting His Witness* (#1515), the latest in her family saga, CAVANAUGH JUSTICE. Here, an undercover cop crosses paths with a secretive beauty who winds up being a witness to a mob killing. And then, can a single mother escape her vengeful ex *and* fall in love with her protector? Find out in Linda Conrad's *Safe with a Stranger* (#1517), the first book in her miniseries, THE SAFEKEEPERS, which weaves family, witchcraft and danger into an exciting read. Finally, crank up your air-conditioning as brand-new author Jill Sorenson raises temperatures with *Dangerous to Touch* (#1518), featuring a psychic heroine and lawman, who work on a murder case and uncover a wild attraction.

This month is all about finding love against the odds and those adventures lurking around every corner. So as you lounge on the beach or in your favorite chair, lose yourself in one of these gems from Silhouette Romantic Suspense!

Sincerely,

Patience Smith
Senior Editor

Killer TEMPTATION

Nina Bruhns

Silhouette®

Romantic
SUSPENSE

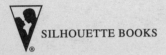

SILHOUETTE BOOKS

ISBN-13: 978-0-373-27586-1
ISBN-10:   0-373-27586-2

KILLER TEMPTATION

NINA BRUHNS

credits her Gypsy great-grandfather for her great love of adventure. Nina has lived and traveled all over the world, including a six-year stint in Sweden. She has been on scientific expeditions from California to Spain to Egypt and Sudan, and has two graduate degrees in archeology (with a specialty in Egyptology). She speaks four languages and she writes a mean hieroglyphic!

But Nina's first love has always been writing. For her, writing for Silhouette Books is the ultimate adventure. Drawing on her many experiences gives her stories a colorful dimension and allows her to create settings and characters out of the ordinary. She has won numerous awards for her previous titles including a prestigious National Readers Choice Award, two Daphne DuMaurier Awards of Excellence for Overall Best Romantic Suspense of the year, five Dorothy Parker Awards and two Golden Heart Awards, among many others.

A native of Canada, Nina grew up in California and currently resides in Charleston, South Carolina, with her husband and three children. She loves to hear from her readers and can be reached at P.O. Box 2216, Summerville, SC 29484-2216 or by e-mail via her Web site, www.NinaBruhns.com, or via the Harlequin Web site, www.eHarlequin.com.

For my fellow SEDUCTION SUMMER authors,
Sheri WhiteFeather and Cindy Dees.
And my wonderful editor, Natashya Wilson.
You ladies are truly a joy to work with!
Here's to many more projects together.
Love, Nina

Chapter 1

Fiji
June, present day

Fiji was totally gorgeous.

Zoë Conrad gazed up at her assignment, a charming, whitewashed Queen Anne-style bed-and-breakfast perched on a vividly green jungle-covered slope above a sparkling blue and white crystalline beach. "Romantic and isolated," the Secret Traveler info sheet had said of the Indigo Inn, which was located on one of the northeastern islands of Fiji. Zoë would definitely add *quaint* and *appealing* to that description. Colorful birds flitted through the trees. Sweet, fragrant flowers scented the air and a pretty sailboat bobbed cheerfully next to the dock where she stood by her luggage, taking it all in.

My God, she thought with an appreciative sigh, everything is perfect. Absolute five-star perfection.

Well. Except for the dead guy in the hammock.

Zoë took one look and screamed at the top of her lungs. The man was sprawled with both arms and one shorts-clad leg dangling over the sides, his Hawaiian shirt covered in blood.

Spinning around on the rickety wooden dock, she jumped up and down, waving her arms hysterically at the swiftly receding seaplane that had just dropped her off in what was supposed to be paradise.

"Wait! Stop!" she yelled as the pontoon craft pointed its nose away from her and taxied smoothly over the turquoise water. "For the love of Pete, stop! *Help!*"

But her friends and fellow Secret Travelers, Alicia and Madeline, who were off to their own assignments, must have thought she was simply waving an enthusiastic goodbye, because they waved back just as enthusiastically from the small, square windows of the six-seater. Then the plane lifted from the waves and soared off into the clear blue sky.

Leaving Zoë all alone with two suitcases and a dead guy.

"Damn," she muttered desperately. *"Damn, damn, damn!"*

Now what? The three-day seminar she'd taken when she'd first joined the company as a hotel-and-resort evaluator two years ago hadn't covered finding dead bodies.

Sticking her shaking hands under her armpits, she

reluctantly turned back to the beautiful bed-and-breakfast on the hill, praying someone would come out to greet her. No such luck. The Indigo Inn's owner, Sean Guthrie, had profusely apologized in his last e-mail that he would most likely be away on business until morning and the new staff would not be arriving for three days. She'd assured him that was quite all right, she'd picked the inn for its solitude, not to be pampered. He'd replied that the front door would be unlocked as usual, the gardener would be there to help her with her luggage and the inn's hostess, Aruna, would return from her afternoon break at four o'clock. Meanwhile there would be sandwiches and beer in the fridge, help herself.

Great.

Not that Zoë couldn't use a beer about now. Or something stronger.

A *lot* stronger.

A pair of scarlet, blue and green parrots swooped down and sat on a tree branch just above the hammock and started chattering gaily above the dead guy's head.

"Shoo!" she yelled at the birds, appalled, and hurried up the garden path to chase them away from the body.

Which, just then, let out a soft grunt.

"Omigod! He's not dead!"

She ran up and peered at the man over the edge of the giant hammock. Could this be the gardener? She held her breath, waiting for him to move. Or do something.

He didn't. He still looked dead. The sigh must have been in her imagination.

She tilted her head in pity. A shame, really. The guy had been handsome—in a stiff sort of way. Okay, *really* handsome. But the tacky—and blood-soaked—tropical shirt did nothing to enhance his bronze tan and the long, sun-streaked hair that curled over its splayed collar. Nor did his mouth, which might well have been kissable when he was still alive, but now hung open in a slack slash of sculpted lips and white teeth.

A muscle in his cheek twitched.

She jumped a foot in the air and squeaked.

He *was* alive!

Heart pounding hard, she leaned farther over him, putting her face close to his, frantically trying to tell if he was breathing or not without actually touching him or the blood.

Strange. He didn't *smell* dead. He smelled…earthy. Like salt spray and male sweat. And…spicy tomatoes. Definitely the gardener.

But he still wasn't breathing.

Oh, God. Panic welled anew within her. Should she give him CPR? She swallowed heavily. Or mouth-to-mouth?

Gross!

Just then, his chest lifted slightly, as though he were trying to breathe but couldn't. *That settled it.*

Gingerly, she slid her hand under his neck and lifted, then with her pulse beating out of control, she put her lips over his and prepared to—

His eyes popped open.

She screamed and tried to scramble away, but her foot slipped. He sucked in a huge breath just as she tumbled face-first into the hammock and landed on his chest. Instantly she felt the front of her chic new sundress soak through with blood. She screamed again.

"What the *hell*—!" was followed by a string of virulent male curses. His arms flailed out and tangled with hers, as did their legs, tipping them both out of the hammock onto a soft, mulch-covered flower bed.

This time he landed on top of her. Stunned, she gaped up at him. A large curvy glass, empty except for a celery stick, rolled out of nowhere, coming to a rest amid the bright red carnations by her elbow. A delicate scent of cloves mingled with the tomato smell.

"Who in blazes are you?" the dead guy asked. He looked really mad. "And what the *hell* do you think you're doing?"

"You were dead!" she exclaimed breathlessly. "Look at you! You're covered in blood! I was only trying to help."

He blinked.

She frowned. "I was about to give you mouth-to-mouth."

He blinked again. Then the corner of his lips curved up just a shade. If she didn't know better she'd say they curved up naughtily. But it must have been from the pain of his wound. That must hurt like hell. It had to. All that blood.

"Okay," he said. Two seconds later he'd spun them so she was on top of him again. He lifted his chin and closed his eyes, but somehow still managed to look expectant. "Go for it."

Her jaw dropped.

That's when she felt his hands on her backside. Smoothing over the slippery silk of her sundress. His fingertips crept along the edge of her thong by her—

"You aren't hurt at all!" she cried accusingly. She

yanked herself up off his chest and looked down at it, searching for a wound of any kind.

Nothing.

All at once she remembered the tall glass. With the celery stick. And the scent of tomatoes.

She gasped in outrage. "Bloody Mary!"

He looked singularly unrepentant. "They call me Breeze, actually. But I do have a great-aunt named Mary, if that helps."

Before she could even think of a retort, his hands cupped her bottom suggestively. "Now, about that mouth-to-mouth…"

As he gazed languorously up at her, she suddenly became aware of his body under hers. It was very male. Solid and powerful. Large.

Growing larger by the second.

Her eyes widened.

They widened even more when he pulled her back down onto his chest, lifted his head and slid his tongue enticingly over her bottom lip.

"Open for me, now," he ordered softly. And kissed her!

She was shocked. She was scandalized. She was also moaning in pleasure. Good lord, the man could kiss!

"Oh, yeah," he murmured, running his hands up and down her body as he kissed her to within an inch of her life. "If this is dead, kill me more."

She tended to agree.

She danced her tongue over his.

She knew her behavior was disgraceful. It was her job to be completely neutral, to remain aloof from the people who ran the establishments she was sent to rate, not to fall into the arms of the first employee she ran across. But what woman could resist a man as sexy as this, who could kiss like a god? Besides, he was only the gardener.

By the time she came to her senses he'd rolled back on top of her, crushing the entire bed of carnations beneath them, and his questing hands had pushed the hem of her dress nearly all the way up her thighs.

Okay, too far. Too fast.

"Wait," she managed to say, shivering a little from the wet silk glued to her chest. Or was it from something else?

Not wanting to think about that too closely, she extracted her fingers from the thick spill of the man's sunstreaked tawny hair and grabbed hold of his broad shoulders. "Wait."

He paused and pulled back just enough to gaze down at her with half-lidded, pleasure-filled eyes. "Something wrong?"

She let out a long breath, attempting to gather her wits and dispel the sensual aura of temptation that surrounded the two of them. "No. Yes." She shook her head in frustration. "I mean, this is um, very um… That is, you're an incredible kisser, but I don't even know your name."

His lips curved in amusement. They looked soft, and slightly moist. "Yeah, you do. I told you, it's Breeze."

So tempting just to—

What? Right. Breeze. *That* should tell her something about the man.

She yanked her gaze from his lips. "Well, you don't know mine, and—"

"What is it?"

But just then his body shifted, making her mortifyingly aware of his position between her legs, and his…enjoyment of being there.

Ho-boy.

She suddenly noticed he had that expectant look again. Um… "What?"

"Your name. What is it?"

She blushed furiously. "Zoë," she said, flustered that he could distract her so easily. "Zoë Conrad."

For a split second his expression froze, then it creased into a smile. "Okay. Well, it's nice to meet you, Zoë."

"You, too, um…Breeze."

"Anyway…"

To his credit, he didn't attempt to continue the encounter, but gave her cheek a chaste kiss and rolled off her, coming to his feet in a single graceful movement. He stretched out his hand to her, grimacing first at her dress then down at his own shirt. "Hell. Spilled that whole damn Bloody Mary. Must have been more tired than I thought. Really sorry about the mess. Naturally I'll replace your dress."

She pulled self-consciously at her red-soaked bodice, hoping he wouldn't notice her nipples were still as hard as cherry stones. "Don't worry about it. It's actually washable."

For a second his eyes lingered on her breasts, then rose. "Guess we better get you up to the house and out of those clothes."

A wave of heat rushed up her throat and through her cheeks. Her face was probably as red as the stain on her dress. "Um…"

He winced. "To wash them, of course."

Ah.

Was that a fleeting touch of disappointment she felt? Good grief, no! Probably just the breeze…er, wind…on the wet fabric.

Rubbing his palms down his jeans, Breeze glanced back toward the dock. "How 'bout if I grab your suitcases and meet you up there?" With that he strode off.

She let out a long, pent-up breath. "Way to go, girl," she muttered. "Very professional. That promotion to the A-team is practically yours." Giving her bodice a last tug, she rolled her eyes and headed for the steps up to the Indigo Inn's front entrance.

Her dream since escaping her parents' small dairy farm in Wisconsin was to build an exciting life for herself…as far away from the boring routine and highly insecure finances of the farm as possible. She'd thought her job with the Secret Traveler would provide that. But so far she'd been stuck on the milk runs, evaluating low-budget motels and hotels in the States for the big-name automobile-touring books. Not that she begrudged her apprenticeship. She'd only worked at the company for two years, and most evaluators put in three to four years before being sent overseas. But the scheduled Fiji team had fallen ill in Indonesia and had to be replaced at the last minute. Zoë, Alicia and Madeline had been in the right place at the right time with their bags packed, and gotten the assignment. This was a career-changing opportunity for all of them to prove they were ready to be an A-team—permanently.

Zoë was *not* going to blow it.

Certainly not for some oversexed gardener. Even if he did kiss like a dream.

No, her job demanded objectivity, professionalism and anonymity in her evaluation of a given accommodation. Kissing the staff definitely did not qualify as any of those.

Good lord. A dead body. Inwardly she cringed. What had she been *thinking?*

But as soon as she climbed the smooth wooden steps to the Indigo Inn's wide verandah, her faux pas was instantly forgotten. She smiled in delight. White wicker rocking chairs, love seats and tables dotted the shady space, which was made even cozier by sweetly fragrant flowering vines twining up the square columns and lush ferns hanging from the framework. White slatted shutters were pinned back at the generous windows, which had no glass to obstruct the breeze that gently ruffled the curtains inside. As promised, the door was wide open. Apparently crime wasn't a big concern on this small island.

She stepped inside and sucked in a gasp of genuine enchantment. In preparation for her visit, she'd read the previous guidebook's rating of the inn. It had not been flattering. At all. *Old*, *run-down* and *falling apart* were some of the more positive adjectives used in the description. But this room was nothing like that. Someone had obviously put a lot of time, hard work and careful attention to detail into a renovation that left her feeling as if she'd stepped into a tropical plantation house from a bygone era of golden luxury.

"What do you think?" asked Breeze from behind her.

"Absolutely lovely," she answered on an appreciative sigh. "It's just beautiful."

"Thanks." He winked as he carried her suitcases to the staircase. "We like it. Come on. I'll show you to your room."

She followed him up the curving staircase into a nice-sized sitting room with a gallery-style balcony that overlooked the jungle slope above.

"Feel free to explore the house," he said. "There won't be any other guests arriving for a few days."

"Oh?" she asked, curious. "Why not?"

"I gave myself a cushion to finish all the renovations before booking solid. I always find things take longer than expected."

"*You* did the work?"

He grinned at her. "If you want something done right—"

"Do it yourself," she completed dryly. If she'd heard the hackneyed phrase once, she'd heard it a million times from her father. Dad was big on doing things himself. Pretty much everything, in fact. Which explained whuy, growing up, she'd hardly ever seen him even though he worked right on the farm they all lived on. "You did an incredible job. But I'm surprised you had time," she observed. "The gardens are also beautiful."

"Here we are," he said, opening the door at the end of the hall to reveal a huge room that was so gorgeous she just stood there gaping. But he didn't give her a chance to take it all in. He dropped her suitcases on the lace-covered, canopied bed and herded her straight into the lavishly appointed bathroom.

"Now," he said, slanting his dark, seductive gaze at her, "take off your clothes."

Chapter 2

The second he said it, Sean could have kicked himself.

What was with his mouth around this woman? It seemed to have a will of its own, ignoring all his brain's orders. His nickname was Breeze, but it should have been Bigfoot. As in *Big Foot in Mouth*.

Zoë Conrad was staring up at him with eyes wide as saucers, and those delectably sweet lips parted just a fraction, as if she were totally scandalized…but also maybe a little tempted to obey.

Wow. *In your dreams, buddy.*

He'd always had a thing for leggy blondes, and Zoë fit the bill perfectly. Her face was, in that typical American way, more wholesomely pretty than beautiful, but her tall, slim curves were definitely a ten. Or better. And the memory of holding all that perfection in his hands was making his palms itch.

He cleared his throat and edged toward the bathroom door. "The washer's down, um—I'll just, uh, wait here outside and you can hand them through to me." Then as an afterthought, he said, "There's a guest robe on the bed if you…" No. Too far away. He shook his head and eased through the door.

Her wide eyes followed his every move. Like a fluffy little kitten might a mountain lion. Innocent, skittish, but also a bit…fascinated?

Right. Make that *Big Imagination*.

He closed the door behind him with a firm *click*.

But damn, if he didn't wish he'd meant his unintentional Freudian slip exactly as she'd interpreted it.

Well, naturally, he did mean it like that. But no way could he act on it. He was the owner of the Indigo Inn, and the one who'd called in a favor from his old San Diego State fraternity brother, Matt Cameron, current CEO of the Secret Traveler, to get a rush job on his evaluation so it would make the upcoming travel guide editions. As a single woman arriving at a B&B that specialized in romantic isolation, chances were good that Zoë was his evaluator.

Damn. He'd been suspicious when she'd requested to come early even though the full staff wouldn't be there for the first few days of her stay. He should have listened to himself.

Seducing her might be considered a blatant attempt at influencing the rating process.

Not that it would matter in the end. Anyone could see the Indigo now rated a solid five stars out of five. Or it would when the rest of the staff reported for duty the day after tomorrow.

So maybe he should just go on back in there and—

The bathroom door opened a tiny crack and she thrust her wadded-up dress at him. "I'm going to take a shower now," she said, and the door smacked closed again.

God, too much information.

Then the lock snicked home. He felt a surge of disappointment.

He was so losing it.

"Okay," he called through the all-too-deliberate barrier, gathering what little dignity he had left. "Help yourself to anything you see. Aruna will be here at four. Cocktails served at sunset on the verandah. Meanwhile I'll be down in the boathouse if you need me…anything."

With that, he left her to her shower and beelined it to the laundry room on the first floor behind the kitchen before he could change his mind. After all, as the little imp who had somehow taken over his libido gleefully reminded him, he did have a master key.

He ground his teeth and spun the washing machine dial to deal with their tomato-soaked clothes. Stripping out of his ratty khaki shorts and Hawaiian shirt—he never wore underwear if he didn't have to—he tossed them in with her dress. He'd meant to change clothes before his very first guest ever arrived, into nice slacks—with BVDs— and an indigo polo, as befitted the owner of the inn.

He glanced around and his stomach sank. What had Anna done with all the guest robes she'd been ironing earlier? Please don't tell him he'd have to walk down to the boathouse *naked*. Yeah, the Indigo was meant to be casual, but that was taking things to the extreme.

Oh, well. So much for first impressions. Hell, he'd pretty much blown that whole scenario anyway, regardless of what he'd been wearing.

He pushed out a breath. He couldn't believe he'd passed out in the hammock like that. Jeez, he hadn't passed out anywhere for any reason since deep in his college days. Certainly never while he'd been married to Her Royal Roxanne. Heaven forbid he should do anything so plebian around his snooty ex-wife.

Okay, sure, he was good and exhausted from three days of chasing around half the South Pacific tracking down that damned couple who'd gone and lost one of his favorite yachts, the *Hasty Breeze,* to try and pry out of them what had really happened to it. And that on top of getting only about four hours sleep a night for the past two weeks while he frantically worked round the clock to get the Indigo ready to receive guests. He'd nearly killed himself for months renovating the property in addition to personally overseeing the upkeep and rental of his fleet of yachts over on the big island of Vanua Levu.

Still. No excuse. He knew how vitally important this Secret Traveler rating was to his business plan, both immediate and long-term. His yacht rentals were doing well, but he really needed his own marina. And that took cash. To get cash he needed solid collateral. That was the Indigo Inn—but it had to be filled year-round with wealthy paying customers. Which in turn demanded a five-star rating to attract them.

So if Zoë Conrad was the person in whose hands his entire business future lay, the word *lay* had no business giving his own hands dangerous ideas.

He sighed. Tell that to his hormones.

Obviously he'd been working too hard lately and gone without for far too long. Too bad there was no possibility of remedying the situation anytime soon.

Ah, the joys of self-employment.

Anyway, if he didn't get some much-needed sleep before sunset cocktails, he was likely to make an even bigger ass of himself and end up face-first in the pitcher of seabreezes.

He was grabbing a bottle of water from the refrigerator before hoofing it down to the boathouse before Zoë got out of the shower when he spotted the welcome basket that was supposed to be in her room. It was sitting on the kitchen table. *Damn.* Aruna must have forgotten to take it up before she left on break. And she wouldn't be back for several hours. By then it would be too late to be much of a welcome.

He glanced down at himself again and cursed, weighing the wisdom of going back upstairs with no clothes on. Not smart. Not smart at all.

But he had to think of that rating—the check box on the form where it asked how welcome the guest had been made to feel. Hell of a welcome she'd had so far. Without the basket, he'd rate a big fat zero on that one. No choice. He had to risk it.

Besides, Zoë was in the shower. He just had to be really fast.

Swiftly he filled an ice bucket, grabbed a couple slips of champagne and the overflowing welcome basket, then zipped up the stairs and knocked. No answer. He peeked into her room. The muffled sound of splashing water came from the bathroom. Excellent.

Striding across to the room's bay window, he quickly deposited the basket on a small antique table nestled in its curve, and slipped the chilled bucket into a special stand next to it. He was just pushing the two slips of Cristal into the ice when the bathroom door opened and Zoë walked out. He halted in midaction.

Her eyes were closed and she was rubbing a thick towel in her wet hair.

And God help him.

She was naked, too.

Sean figured he had three choices: run like hell, hide under the bed, or brazen it out. And about a nanosecond to choose.

He swore under his breath. Her eyes popped open. *Too late*.

If he'd thought they'd been wide before, he was wrong. And when they landed on his—on him—they got even wider.

Okay. Brazen it was.

Somehow he produced a grin, and hoped *he* didn't get wider. *Like there was a prayer of that not happening*.

He forced a chuckle. "We've got to stop meeting like this."

All at once she gasped, as though she'd just realized she was as naked as he was, yanked her towel from her hair and covered her front with it.

Way too late.

"Wh-What are you d-doing here?" she stammered.

He gave one of the pint-sized champagne bottles an artful twist in the ice. *Brazen,* he reminded himself.

"Just our way of welcoming you to the Indigo Inn." He smiled to cover an inward wince.

"B-but you're naked!"

He winked. "So are you."

Her mouth dropped open but she didn't say a word. Just backed off to let him pass when he said, "Enjoy the goodies," and headed for the door. He strolled out casually, as though it was the most natural thing in the world for him to deliver baskets to his guests with no clothes on.

Once out in the hall, he closed the door and leaned gingerly against it, letting out a long breath.

Definitely brazen.

Zoë stood frozen to the spot for a few seconds, then launched herself at the bed and scrambled into the blue silk robe that was decoratively arranged on the lacy white spread.

The man really had some brass—

She slammed her eyes shut. *Okay, wrong analogy*.

Then she had a horrible thought. Good grief. Was this place a *nudist* colony? Grabbing the brochure on the nightstand, she scanned through the entire four pages twice. No mention of nudity or naturist leanings in the inn's description. *Whew*. But then what possible explanation—

All at once a rush of relief spilled through her. Oh! Of course he must have put his clothes in with hers to be washed. And she had told him she was showering… That must be it.

Her composure somewhat recovered, she wrapped the robe securely around her and went over to the table. Well, at least he'd brought champagne. And the striking woven basket was filled with a cornucopia of exotic fruits, chocolates, biscuits and other tasty delights. Sitting on top was a crystal flute etched with Welcome to the Indigo Inn. She touched the delicate rim. Lifting the accompanying split of bubbly from the ice bucket, she read the label. Cristal. Very nice, indeed.

It was all absolutely beautiful. Full points for feeling welcomed.

Despite the unorthodox delivery. She giggled softly. She might just forgive him that, though.

Unable to help herself, she glanced out the curved bay window. Breeze was hurrying down the brick path toward a charming wooden cottage with thatched roof that was built on stilts over the water next to the dock. The boathouse? Did he live there? As she watched, he took the stairs leading up to the upper level of the small structure two at a time. Still naked as a jaybird. Pulling open the door, he turned and gave her a cheerful wave, then disappeared inside.

She gave a surprised laugh. How had he known she would be watching? Was she that predictable? Or did he just have that big an ego?

In truth, she didn't know whether to be more shocked or amused by the man. If nothing else, the guy was certainly an original.

He was also entitled to that ego. Lord, he was even more gorgeous in the buff than he had been rolling around in the flower bed kissing her....

Fanning her face at *that* memory, she turned determinedly away from the window.

Enough of this nonsense. She wasn't here to daydream about handsome men. And certainly not to roll around with them in flower beds. Or ogle them.

She was here to do a job. Just that. Nothing else.

Setting aside all thoughts of the hunky naked gardener, she slipped on a fresh dress—this time a flirty-skirted halter style in a yummy shade of coral that looked great against the light honey tan she'd managed to acquire recently rating motels in Texas—combed her wet hair and brushed on a little makeup. Then, taking Breeze's invitation at face value, she pulled out her thick Secret Traveler notebook and systematically inspected the Indigo Inn, filling in the required stats for her guidebook rating.

When she'd first gotten this assignment she'd been more than a little nervous because her boss had told her the owner, Sean Guthrie, was a personal friend of his. He'd also said Guthrie never, ever did anything halfway, so he expected the place to be knock-your-socks-off fabulous. Zoë had interpreted his enthusiasm to mean she'd better come in with a high rating or she could kiss her promotion to the A-team goodbye. But Zoë had always been scrupulously honest in her evaluations. She didn't plan to change that, not even for a personal friend of the boss. So, inwardly she'd been terrified the Indigo Inn wouldn't match up to her employer's superlative expectations.

But in fact, the luxurious bed-and-breakfast far surpassed anything either of them had imagined. The rooms were splendid and expansive, the furnishings rich and the appointments lavish. If the guest services were even half as good, a high rating would be no problem.

Provided there were no more little…incidents… with the staff. The tone and atmosphere of a given accommodation was just as important as the physical surroundings. So far it had been just a tad too…unpredictable… for five stars.

However, the rest of the afternoon went very well. She explored every nook and cranny of the Indigo Inn and loved it all. Even better, before the inn's hostess arrived back from her break, Zoë was nearly finished filling in the endless rating forms. Sometimes it took her days to casually acquire all the needed info without her cover being blown. But now with the busywork done, all she had to do was sit back, relax, sample and observe.

Tucking the notebook back in the bottom of her suitcase, she felt a big smile on her face and joy in her heart.

Fiji was *so* much better than Texas.

And with this assignment, her luck was finally turning. At last, her life was taking off in the direction she wanted. Thrills. Excitement. Adventure.

That's what she was talking about.

This job on Fiji was her ticket to ride. Nothing short of a disaster could prevent her dreams from coming true.

And a disaster was *not* going to happen. Not here. Not to her. Not this time.

Not a chance.

Even a dead guy couldn't stop her now.

Chapter 3

Sean made sure he was awake, dressed in a casual but nice shirt and khaki shorts, and standing behind the bar on the verandah as the sun was about to dip below the horizon and Zoë came down for cocktails. She seemed surprised to see him. And a bit embarrassed.

Damn, she was cute when she blushed.

"Well, at least you're alive and fully clothed," she said as she sauntered over to him. They were alone, since Aruna was in the kitchen putting last touches on the special dishes she was preparing for later tonight.

"Hell, the night is young," he responded with a wink, and tried not to remember how Zoë had looked when *she* wasn't fully clothed. Although the dress she was wearing was nearly as good. "Any minute now I could be shot down where I stand."

She chuckled. "Oh, I think you're safe enough. Providing you're any good at mixing drinks." She drew a finger lazily through the condensation on the icy glass pitcher he was stirring. He felt it all the way down his spine. "What have you got here?"

"Seabreezes."

She glanced up and gave him a grin. "Cute."

He grinned back. "So I've been told."

Her blue eyes rolled. But she was laughing. Good. Maybe the day wasn't a total disaster.

"And modest, too."

"Positively humble," he agreed. "Can I pour you one? Or would you rather have something else?"

"What the heck. I'll give your concoction a try."

Under her watchful gaze he poured the cranberry-colored liquid into an oversized martini glass. Technically he should be using a Collins glass, but he liked the stylish look of the martinis better. Call him a rebel.

He added a twist and cranberry impaled on a swizzle stick along with a tiny blue umbrella, and handed her the glass. "Live dangerously I always say."

When he held on just a tad too long, her eyes met his. Flustered again. "So I've noticed."

God, she was turning him on. He had to catch himself before he leaned in for another of her mouth-watering kisses.

No, no, no, he reminded himself for the hundredth time. *Just business, Breeze.*

But damn, why did the only woman he'd been seriously attracted to in years have to be the one woman he couldn't—shouldn't, anyway—make a move on?

He let go of the glass and took the opportunity to

chastise his raging libido. "Right. Look, Zoë…about this afternoon. I want to apologize. For everything. There's no excuse, but when you arrived I'd been up for almost thirty-six hours straight and was a brainless zombie. That's why I'd passed out cold and…um…had impaired judgment while you were in the shower. I'm really sorry for my outrageous behavior."

"Not to worry." She smiled and wandered over to the porch swing. "It was kind of exciting, really. I mean finding a dead body," she quickly added. "Made me feel like I was in one of those cable TV movies. *Murder in the South Seas.*"

"Gee, thanks." After pouring himself a seabreeze—no umbrella—he strolled over to lean against the railing in front of the swing where she'd taken a seat. "Say… Doesn't the girl usually fall in love with the rugged bush pilot in those things? Or the suave policeman? Or the mysterious owner of the bed-and-breakfast where she's staying?" He waggled his eyebrows.

She choked on her drink. "Uh, no. The bush pilot is always a drug dealer and the cop is corrupt. Everyone knows that."

He grinned. "And the mysterious owner of the B and B?"

"The bad guy," she said without hesitation.

He gave a bark of laughter. "But before she finds out, she always has hot monkey sex on the beach with him, right?"

She gave a smirk. "Yeah, but then she's forced to shoot him in the kneecap and turn him in."

"Ouch." He winced. "Don't get any ideas."

Her smirk went lopsided. "Trust me, you have plenty

of those for both of us." But her blue eyes were sparkling like the ocean on a bright day. If he weren't already smitten, those eyes would have done it for sure.

Hell, she was smart, sassy, her legs went on for miles in that sundress she was almost wearing, and she had a sense of humor, too. What more could a man ask for?

When he just stood there grinning like a fool, she added, "Besides, you're safe. You're just the gardener."

Before he could recover his faculties and correct her, the Indigo's two obnoxious resident parrots swooped through the verandah and landed on the decorative woodwork on one end, chattering like the pests they were.

"Beat it," he told them with a wave. "No handouts tonight."

"They live here?" Zoë asked, looking charmed. Figured. They were such con artists. "Do they have names?"

"Scarlett and Rhett. And don't even think about feeding them," he grumbled. "They'll find a way into your luggage and you'll never be rid of the little beggars."

She grinned widely. "I'll have you know, Scarlett and Rhett looked very upset when we all thought you were dead."

"Probably just worried about where their next free meal will come from," he retorted, eyeing them with annoyance.

She laughed. "Still, they are gorgeous."

Yeah, he used to think so, too. Which is how he'd ended up with the freeloaders. When he'd first arrived at the Indigo, he'd fallen for their exotic scarlet, blue and green plumage and big innocent eyes, and had made the mistake of feeding them. Now they were eating him out of house and home, and if Aruna forgot to fill the feeder before leaving, they'd wake him at the crack of dawn outside his window with their infernal squawking and wouldn't shut up until he'd trudged all the way up from the boathouse and filled it *and* left treats to make up for the oversight.

"Looks can be deceiving," he muttered.

Suddenly, Aruna ran out onto the verandah in a rush of smiles and colorful skirts.

"The food for the celebration is all packed and ready, Mr. Breeze," she said breathlessly in her melodic Fijian accent. "Sure you won't need my help carrying?"

For a second he was confused, then remembered again. There was a big to-do planned this evening in the village, and he and Zoë were invited. Aruna was one of the *meke* dancers.

"Heavens no," he said. "We'll manage just fine. You go on now. I know you have a lot to do to prepare."

"I just hope the night will not be spoiled. Big trouble brews in the village," Aruna said animatedly. Her plump hands fluttered in the air, making Scarlett and Rhett flap their wings. "The chief's favorite niece, Jeela, last week she was supposed to be visiting her cousins on Taveuni. But yesterday everyone find out, five days ago she elopes with a boy, Wilson Taani. He is a fisherman from Maruiti Island," she declared, clearly aghast.

Everything was always a drama in the village. Sean chalked it up to no TV reception. However, he did recall hearing something about a vicious historical rivalry between the two islands. Sort of a Hatfields-and-McCoys situation.

"I take it that's not good."

"Terrible, terrible thing. What will they do? Where will they live? What about the children? Oh, very bad."

"Well, then you must go help sort it out." Aruna wasn't exactly an elder, but she was very wise and practical, and well-respected in the village.

"I will, and— Oh! I forgot my *salusalu*," she cried, and vanished back inside.

He turned to Zoë. "That's a flower lei," he explained at her puzzled look. Then added, "Tonight we'll be eating—"

But before he could finish, Aruna sailed back through the front door, this time with a beautiful flower garland around her neck. "I'll be going now, Mr. Breeze, Miss Zoë. See you up there."

"Break a leg, Aruna."

Giving him an exasperated but affectionate smile, she hurried down the steps to the trail that ran northward along the shore.

"Up where?" Zoë asked. "What's going on?"

"In the island village at the foot of the old volcano." He swept his hand to the distinctive conical mountain behind the inn. "It's the chief's birthday today and there is a gala celebration planned, complete with a *lovo*—a big feast—and a *meke*, which is a traditional Fijian dance. Very festive." He shook his head. "I hope this elopement doesn't put a crimp in things."

"Why would it?"

"Fijians take family and marriage very seriously.

The couple could easily find themselves ostracized from both islands."

"How awful. Surely there must be a way to prevent it."

"Timing their elopement to coincide with the chief's birthday feast was clever. He'll no doubt do something to smooth things over between the families. Anyway, we've both been invited to the celebration. Would you like to go?"

Her face lit with interest. "I'd love to. You'll have to tell me all about it."

"Absolutely. But first we watch the sunset."

He turned to the kaleidoscope playing over the ocean surface, which was the reason he'd decided to schedule cocktails on the verandah for his guests at precisely this time of day. He went to stand next to the swing where she was slowly pushing herself back and forth.

The sun was a blazing ball of orange, already cut in half by a vivid swath of yellows and reds.

"Spectacular, isn't it?"

"I'll say," she whispered.

As it slowly descended into the deep blue of the sea, they fell into a reverent silence. Long moments later, the last sliver of shimmering gold melted to indigo, and shades of dusk enveloped the island.

"That was amazing," Zoë said.

Her words brought Sean back with a start and he realized something even more amazing. For five whole minutes he'd been totally relaxed, his mind comfortably blank of the many responsibilities and worries he carried around with him constantly, some nights even in his sleep.

"Yes. Incredible," he agreed, focusing his attention back on Zoë.

And once again he was struck by her quiet attractiveness. Her pale shoulders, highlighted by the halter style of her dress, were lovely. An image of them peeking out from behind the towel this afternoon, spangled with droplets of water from her shower, went through him like a shiver. He'd wanted to slide his hands over them, to touch her soft skin, to feel her delicate feminine curves and continue downward until he'd felt every curve of her lush body. He still did.

Damn it, how was he ever going to spend an entire evening around her, with the memory of her lithe, naked form burned into his retinas, and not touch her?

Her gaze lingered on the horizon, her expression filled with awe. Kind of like the way she'd looked at him earlier when *he* was naked.

Aw, hell.

This was ridiculous.

Perhaps he should reevaluate the whole off-limits deal. Despite his suspicions, he really didn't know for certain that she had been sent by the Secret Traveler. What if the evaluator was someone totally different, and he missed the opportunity for a fantastic few days with Zoë?

Yes, it merited reconsideration.

He cleared his throat and glanced at his watch. "We should probably get going. It's about two miles to the village and we don't want to be late. You don't mind walking, do you?"

"Not at all. I could use the exercise," she said, rising from the swing. "The plane trip over was brutal. Almost twenty hours."

He looked at her in consternation. "I'm such an idiot. You must be exhausted, and here I am making you—"

She waved him off. "Are you kidding? I can sleep anytime. How often will I get to see a real Fijian dance?" She glanced down at her attire. "But am I dressed appropriately? Should I—"

"Don't you dare. You're fine. More than fine."

His eyes met hers and she must have seen something in them because she swallowed and said, "Okay."

But in the meantime his mind had once again emptied of all thought. All except the one about kissing her.

"Should I bring anything?" she asked.

"Where?"

She blinked. "The ceremony."

He blinked back. *Right. The village.* "Um, no. Wait, yes." He shook his head to clear it. "Food. We need to bring the special dishes Aruna prepared. They're in the kitchen. I'll get them."

Boy, he was in worse trouble than he thought.

All the way to the kitchen he debated hotly with himself. Should he? Shouldn't he? Clearly he would be a basket case if he didn't. He already *was* a basket case.

The question was, if he did give in to this crazy impulse, would he live to bitterly regret it? If Zoë was his Secret Traveler, could he trust her to keep business separate from pleasure? The last woman he'd trusted with anything remotely important had ruined his finances for years and handed him his head on a platter. Not to mention his heart.

Not that his heart would be involved in this affair.

Or his head, obviously. No, he'd stick strictly to other body parts. It was the trust he was really worried about. The one thing he couldn't control.

This was such a bad idea. How could he even be thinking about risking his whole future over a simple case of lust?

Pure insanity.

And yet…damn it, he wanted to in the worst way.

With a sigh, he gathered a few things in a bag, then grabbed the swinging handles of the two covered pots, which Aruna had duct-taped securely shut so the contents wouldn't spill in transit, and strode from the kitchen back out to the verandah. Stepping outside he suddenly caught sight of Zoë's shoes in the soft light from the porch lamps he'd switched on on his way out. They had low, spiky heels and a multitude of delicate straps. Very sexy. But not terribly practical for walking in.

"Your pretty sandals will be ruined for sure. Got any flip-flops?"

She followed his gaze down to her toes and wiggled them. "In my room."

"Better change. But not the dress!" he called after her when she nodded and went inside.

She came out wearing the same knockout outfit, but with sand-colored flip-flops with clear straps so it looked almost as if she was barefoot. Then he led her through the growing darkness down to a well-worn path that wandered along the shore where the white sand met the verdant jungle. It was the easiest route to the village, if not the shortest, and just wide enough for the two of them to walk side-by-side, although the large pots dangling from each hand took some maneuvering not to whack her in the thigh.

"Let me carry one," she offered.

"No way. But you can carry the bag," he said.

"What's in it?" she asked as she lifted it from his shoulder.

"Our gifts for the chief, plus a *sulu* for each of us to wear at the ceremony." He anticipated her next question and said, "That's a kind of sarong."

There was a pause. "You're wearing a skirt?" A touch of amusement colored her voice. "I can't wait."

"Watch it."

They hadn't walked more than a few hundred yards when suddenly there was a rustle in the foliage next to them and the scream of what sounded like a fierce animal.

"What's that?" Zoë grabbed his arm and scrambled behind him. She peered nervously through the thick leaves and vines that grew like they wanted to take over the trail.

"Damn parrots," he muttered. "Nothing to be nervous about."

"You're telling me that sound came from a parrot? It sounded more like a tiger or a bear!"

"None of those on Fiji," he assured her. "Just a couple of feathered jokers—and a former owner with a majorly twisted sense of humor. Their repertoire is endless."

She looked dubious, and still a little scared. He really wanted to put his arm around her and pull her close to reassure her. Damn pots.

"They probably smell the food and are trying to get

me to drop it," he said, hefting one. "Aruna's a great cook and they know it. Once you taste her meals you'll never want to leave." Before he thought better of it, he said, "Which wouldn't be so bad, come to think of it."

Damn.

This really had to stop.

Maybe he'd get lucky and one of the villagers would know where his missing yacht was and he'd have to leave and go get it. Immediately. Like tonight. Before he lost his mind and did something he'd regret.

Or didn't regret but should.

God, he was messed up.

So instead of thinking about how nice Zoë Conrad smelled walking next to him, or how nice she looked in her coral-colored sundress, or how much nicer she would look *not* in her coral-colored sundress, he forced himself to talk about the celebration, and tell her all about the traditional Fijian feast and dancing and rituals she would witness there.

As they talked, the path took them along the edge of the sea where the last reaches of warm ocean waves lapped at their toes. A fingernail of moon rose in the dark sky and reflected like a thin line of silver foil off the indigo water. Their trail skirted around a small, hidden lagoon that was Sean's favorite swimming spot, and past a tide pool that stretched on for a quarter mile and during the day was chock-full of interesting creatures. Then the path turned abruptly inland at a giant black rock sitting in the surf that was a rookery for vast flocks of seabirds, their wings now still and silent as they slept in one huddled, secure mass of glowing white.

"Almost there," he told her as they started up a stretch of semisteep path that would end at the entrance to the village, which was nestled at the foot of the old volcano. When they got to the top of a rise just below the distinctive *lali* hut that sheltered the large drum used to call the islanders together, he halted.

"Before we enter the village we should put on our *sulu*s. To show respect for the chief." He pulled two colorful lengths of cloth from the bag she had carried, and handed her one. "Here."

She looked on as he expertly wound his around his hips over his shorts, made a couple pleats and tucked in the end. "You're going to have to help," she said, frowning. "I'll get mine hopelessly tangled."

"No problem." But as soon as he took the *sulu* from her hand and put his arms around her to wrap it, he knew he'd made a mistake.

She was too close, too warm, smelled too good, to resist forgetting all about the *sulu* and tightening his arms to pull her close instead. He didn't want to be putting more clothes on her, he wanted to be taking off the ones she was wearing.

"Breeze," she said softly into his throat as he battled with himself not to make things worse and kiss her.

He pretended to be fussing with the *sulu*, vainly attempting to wrap it around her backside without letting her go. "Yeah?"

"What are you doing?"

"Trying to resist you."

There was a pause before she said, "How's that working out?"

"Not so great."

She moved against him, her breasts pillowing into his chest. He almost groaned.

"Maybe I should try tying the *sulu* myself."

"No. I can get it."

"I think you'll have to let go to do that." But oddly, her arms crept over his shoulders and around his neck.

"Yeah." He bunched the cloth into one hand and drilled the fingers of his other hand into her mass of golden hair, tilting her face up to his. He stared down at her, filling with a strange wash of guilt mixed with utter longing.

"Don't get involved with me, Zoë."

"Don't worry, I won't," she whispered. "I can't."

"Good. I'm really a mess right now and not a good risk."

"That's fine, because I'm not interested in getting involved." Her mouth edged closer. "With anyone."

He leaned down a fraction. "Good."

"My job comes first," she murmured. "Always."

"Mine, too."

"Good."

"Good," they echoed together, but they were also slowly drowning in each other's eyes.

Then their lips touched. Almost by accident. But after that it was all over. He opened his mouth and devoured her. He tightened his fist in her hair and kissed her and kissed her, licking her, thrusting his tongue into her, biting at her lips and swallowing the moans that surfaced from deep in her throat as her fingers clutched at him.

And when he thought with desperation that if he didn't rip her clothes off *immediately* and plunge into her *right now*, he'd die, he pulled back.

"Good," he whispered, gulping down breaths to steady himself. To calm the hammering of his heart. And the chaos of his mind.

"Yeah," she said. "Good."

"Just so we're clear," he said.

"We are," she said. "Perfectly."

"Okay, then."

So with shaking fingers he tied her *sulu*, picked up the two pots of food and led her past the *lali* hut into the noisy throng of villagers that had gathered for the celebration.

And wished to hell he knew what had just happened.

And even more, what would happen next.

Chapter 4

Okay, wow.

Not good.

No, *too* good.

Amazingly good.

Zoë couldn't think straight. She stumbled, and Breeze caught her arm.

"You okay?"

She tried to speak but couldn't squeeze a single sound past the acute dryness in her throat. Which was somewhat surprising considering the amount of spit they'd just swapped.

She nodded instead.

Smooth.

Breeze didn't smile, just readjusted his grip on her arm and tugged her into a walk, following a large man wearing a *sulu* who must have taken the two pots from him at some point because they were now hanging from the man's two meaty fists. Which left Breeze free to hold her up so she wouldn't fall flat on her face. Grateful for small favors.

Good lord. She was fourteen all over again. Except no one had ever kissed her like that when she was fourteen. Thank God. It was hard enough as a grown-up to deal with a kiss that powerful.

Focus. She had to focus. On something other than the man who'd just kissed her to within an inch of her life.

She took a deep breath and looked around as they walked into the village. Their guide had disappeared with the pots, and if anyone had seen the kiss, they gave no indication. She and Breeze were being swept along in a crowd of people heading toward a large clearing in the center of a cluster of traditional Fijian houses with woven walls and thatched roofs.

Above it all, the shadowy silhouette of the old volcano loomed, illuminated from below by flickering torchlight and from above by the dim rays of the rising moon. The whole thing should have felt creepy, but it didn't. If anything, it felt…cozy. Like the ancient crater was the village's benign protector, and the thick, verdant jungle its warm, comforting blanket.

All so different from the rolling, muddy pastures of the Wisconsin farm and the coldly impersonal glass-and-cement skyscrapers of Chicago.

"Welcome! Welcome!" a jolly male voice greeted them loudly. Immediately she and Breeze were embraced by a strong set of arms belonging to a stocky, gray-haired man with crinkles around his eyes and a wide smile to go with them. After they'd been thoroughly hugged, he boomed at Breeze, "Aruna said you and your guest would join us in celebrating my birthday. I am so glad you made it back in time."

"It is our honor to be here, Chief Katani," Breeze replied, bowing formally as he handed the chief two carefully wrapped gifts that he produced from the bag they'd brought. "Thank you for your generous invitation."

"You are most welcome." The chief waved his hand and they were both festooned with gorgeous, fragrant flower leis. Then he turned to her. "Now introduce me to your lovely lady."

Zoë did her best to follow Breeze's lead during the following complicated introductions to Chief Katani, his family and entourage, and the scores of others who gathered around to greet Breeze heartily and peer at her with curiosity. He seemed to know everyone, and they all seemed to like him tremendously.

But she got the impression of an undercurrent, a buzz of tense conversation held behind hands that seemed at odds with the festive atmosphere. She kept hearing the names Jeela and Wilson spoken in taut undertones. The couple that had eloped. Poor kids. She had a feeling there would be a hunting party tomorrow, and it wouldn't be going after wild game.

She and Breeze were ushered over to a beautifully decorated dance area, around which dozens of elaborately woven mats formed a huge circle on the grassy ground. Burning tiki torches were stuck into the ground everywhere, throwing the meadow and the villagers into a moving kaleidoscope of shadow.

Bowls of exotic-smelling flowers had been placed on the mats. Large wooden trays of food were being carried in by brightly dressed women to the enthusiastic applause of the villagers, who were taking their places cross-legged on the mats. Tray after tray was brought in, of seafood, chicken, taro and cassava, all still wrapped in the leaves in which they'd been buried in big pits and cooked. Everything smelled heavenly.

"Perfect timing," Breeze said. He paused for a moment, then asked, "Sure you're okay?"

She glanced up into his eyes. In them she saw a dash of concern…along with a simmering ember of the heat they'd just shared.

"I could use another seabreeze," she confessed, the embers within her own body flaring to life. What she really wanted was another of his mind-numbing kisses. Or two. Why not three? Maybe a hundred.

He touched her bottom lip with his thumb. "Later," he murmured as though he knew exactly what she was thinking, and she felt the impact of that promise like a spring coiling tight inside her.

But she didn't get a chance to think about what he might have meant by it, because just then they were invited by the chief's wife to take their places as his special guests at the head mat, and the birthday celebration began.

"No seabreezes," Breeze whispered, pointing to a large, carved wooden bowl at the center of the mat, "but there's always the *yaqona*."

"What's that?" she asked, slightly alarmed at the sight of a thick layer of brown powder at the bottom of the bowl.

"In English, kava. Not alcoholic, but it has some interesting effects."

The chief took his seat at the mat, and an official-looking man wearing a colorful shirt, *sulu* and *salu-salu*—Breeze whispered he was a lawyer who lived in the village but practiced over on the big island—approached and clapped his hands at two equally colorfully dressed women, who poured water over the brown powder in the bowl and mixed it together. After adjusting and tasting the brew several times, the man finally nodded, and the women strained the liquid through a cloth into a half-coconut shell. It looked like muddy dishwater. With much ceremony and respect, the coconut shell was presented to the chief, who drained it in a single draught. When he held it up, everyone shouted and clapped. Then the shell was refilled and passed one at a time to each of several men at their mat, ending with Breeze. She cringed inwardly, but he drank it down and didn't appear the least bit grossed out. Afterward, everyone gave a big cheer and dug in to the food.

Zoë tilted her head and took him in with a new respect. No doubt it was a great honor to be included in the *yaqona* ceremony at the head mat. The man they called Breeze obviously had hidden depths. What was his story? And what was his real name, anyway?

He handed her a filled coconut shell. "Drink. If I have to, so do you."

She wrinkled her nose. Honor or not, it looked disgusting. "Are you kidding?"

"If you don't, it'll be an insult," he said without breaking his smile.

Okay, then. She drank. It wasn't bad. Not great, either. Kind of like slightly bitter herbal tea. It made her lips and tongue tingle.

"Good girl," he said approvingly, and for a split second he glanced down at her lips, then looked up again. "Now for some sustenance. The speeches are about to start."

He grabbed their two wooden plates and filled them with a bit of everything, and topped up her coconut shell. She was actually getting used to that *yaqona* stuff.

The speeches were endless, and in Fijian. She pretended to pay attention. Honestly. But when they were over, the conversation around the mat was also mostly in Fijian. To her surprise Breeze spoke the language. Still, by the time she was on her second plate and third coconut shell she was feeling pretty good. Relaxed. Okay, her tongue was completely numb. But the food nevertheless tasted delicious, and really, who cared about understanding the language? All she wanted was to savor the sight and feel of the man sitting next to her. Unlike her tongue, her skin felt extra sensitized.

So she sat there smiling and enjoying it every time her bare shoulder accidentally bumped into his muscular bicep.

Dangerous, she thought.

Very dangerous.

But his body was strong and solid as it brushed against hers, his scent masculine and alluring just below the sweet, spicy aroma of the meal.

His body had felt really good pressed up against her as he'd kissed her earlier. So amazingly good. Seriously, who could concentrate on conversation and dancing when the memory of that kiss permeated her mind like an addictive drug, luring her back to it again and again? Sometimes at the most inappropriate moments… Like when, during one of the dances, he leaned in close to her and whispered, "I need to go talk to someone. Will you be all right on your own for a few minutes?" and she almost reached up and kissed him on the mouth right there in front of everyone. She'd stopped herself just in time.

Yep. *Way* too dangerous.

She had to get hold of herself. Quickly. Or she was liable to do something very, very stupid.

She had to think about the job she was here to do. Her career. Her future. *Not his treacherous kisses.* She had to be cool, calm, objective. Businesslike. Professional.

Yeah. All that.

And besides, she didn't *do* stuff like this. She didn't have affairs. Vacation sex. One-night stands. The few times she'd become intimate with a man it was because he meant something to her. Because they had a relationship.

But she didn't *want* a relationship. Not now, when her career was finally going places. Certainly not with a gardener half a world away from home with no possibility of a future even if they wanted one.

So when he came back, she smiled cheerfully and asked in her most chipper I'm-*so*-not-thinking-about-that-kiss voice, "Did you find who you needed to talk to?"

"Yep," he said, looking grim but trying to hide it below his own smile.

Hello?

Her chipper wilted a little. "Something wrong?"

"Nothing you need to worry about."

"But *you're* worried," she said, wondering what had caused the sudden change in him. "Has something happened at the inn?"

His mouth turned down. "Nah. Just a missing yacht." He flicked a hand. "Old news. I'd hoped one of my friends here might have picked something up on the jungle telegraph about its whereabouts."

"A yacht?"

"One of the charter boats I own."

She filed away her surprise over the fact that he owned charter boats—plural—for later. "And it's missing?"

"The American couple that rented it last week *mislaid* it. At least, that's their excuse."

She looked at him, perplexed. "How on earth do you mislay a boat?"

"That's what I asked. Several times. Very loudly, apparently. In the bar over on Qamea Island where I finally tracked them down." He gave a shrug that would have done a Frenchman proud. "Threats were made. Hell, I wanted to strangle the pair of them." He sighed. "The bartender called security on me."

"Oh, dear."

He gave her a self-deprecating smile. "Bad judgment on my part. I should have known better. I'd been searching for them day and night for two days, and was exhausted. You know me when I'm exhausted. Not a pretty sight."

"Oh, I don't know," she said without thinking. And felt her face go hot, which drew a smile from him.

He touched her chin. "Anyone tell you lately how sweet you are?"

"Not really," she managed, getting dizzy from the look in his eyes.

"Well, you are. What do you say we get out of here, sweet thing?" he asked softly, though the dancing was going strong.

No, *he* was the sweet one, trying to act like nothing was wrong, but she could see he was still upset about his boat. His blue eyes were stormy as he gazed down at her, shooting flames of orange that weren't all from the reflected tiki torches.

She licked her lips and nodded.

And for some reason, her heart pounded louder than the *derua* drums that accompanied the dancing when she answered, "Sure."

It was a proven fact that when Sean Guthrie made up his mind he wanted something, he always got it. Always.

And two minutes ago, Sean had made up his mind. About Zoë.

After he thanked Chief Katani and made their excuses, he grabbed her hand and zigzagged a path through the maze of mats and feasting villagers, nudging his way through the people that milled around the edges.

Straight to the boathouse. No detours.

She stuck close behind him—so close he could feel the warmth of her body radiate against his back. He liked that. Every few feet she'd jostle up against him, and his flesh would burn from the contact. *Anticipation.*

They'd almost made it back down to the *lali* hut and the head of the beach trail home when shouting erupted from behind one of the thatched village houses. A tangle of young men rolled onto the path in front of them, fists flying.

Sean put out a hand to keep Zoë safely behind his back. "Hey!" he said sharply to the youths. "Show some respect!"

The ball of flesh dissolved into legs, arms and torsos as it broke apart and three sturdy twenty-somethings stood up, staring at the ground in shame. It was not appropriate behavior to fight on the chief's birthday.

Sean recognized all three. One was the younger brother of the girl who had eloped, one her older brother.

"What's going on?" he asked. Like he didn't know.

"George insulted Jeela," the younger one said angrily, jabbing a thumb at the third man's chest.

"I was trying to stop the fight," the older brother said. "Jeela was promised to George," he added, wiping blood from his nose.

Sean shook his head in sympathy at the jilted man. "It appears she's made a different choice, mate. Nothing to fight about. My advice is just get over it."

The three stared at the ground again, shuffling their feet uncomfortably. Sean had made no secret of his rocky past, and divorce was still regarded as awkward here. So was being dumped.

George scowled. "But my honor—"

"Screw your honor. Do you really want a wife who's betrayed you in bed with someone else?" Sean sure as hell hadn't.

George's jaw clenched.

Sean reached out to put his hand on the young man's shoulder and tried not to sound bitter. "Good riddance and forget her. Get drunk. Take one of my boats and go fishing. Just don't do anything foolish. Violence is never worth the price."

Clearly battling his fury, George sucked down a calming breath and reluctantly nodded. Jeela's brothers' smiles were strained but genuine as they slapped him on the back. "We'll go fishing with you," they told him. "Our family is shamed, too, you know."

An annoyed feminine voice broke the male solidarity. "She must love him very much."

Surprised, the three others glanced behind him. Sean turned as well. Zoë's arms were folded over her chest, looking at them all like they were missing some big, important point.

Right. He barely resisted snorting. "Love?" he muttered, brow raised in incredulity.

"To leave the village, to have upset her family like this. She must be very much in love."

He wasn't about to argue. Not about *that* subject. And certainly not with a woman.

The three younger men smiled through their teeth, mumbled something and hurried off in the opposite direction. Smart lads.

"Whatever," Sean said, once again pointing his feet back toward home. "Let's go." He was in a hurry.

He just couldn't quite remember why.

Following, she wisely didn't say anything more on the distasteful subject of love and marriage. But when he reached for her hand she kept her arms banded firmly across her abdomen.

Suddenly he remembered why he was in a hurry.
Aw, damn.

The moon had risen about a third of the way up the night sky, lighting the path in patches as he and Zoë descended into the short stand of thick jungle that lay between the village and the ocean. The little-used trail was steep and crisscrossed with roots, and the foliage so dark Sean could barely see the path. He threaded his arm around Zoë's waist to help her navigate. Immediately her body went stiff.

"What?" he asked, peering down at her.

"I'm good on my own," she said.

"It's treacherous here. I don't want you getting hurt." She blinked up at him wordlessly. "You're wearing flip-flops," he reminded her, then realized they were also still wearing their *sulus*. "And let's get out of these," he said, unwinding his own to stuff it into the carry bag. "Easier to walk without the long skirts."

He heard her breath push out. "Fine." She took hers off and thrust it at him, then turned and started walking down the path on her own. He reached for her but she pulled away.

"Zoë, what's wrong?" he asked, grabbing her so this time she couldn't get away from him.

When she tugged her hand and he wouldn't let go, she huffed. "I can't believe how all four of you men blamed her."

"What are you talking about?"

"Jeela. Not one of you tried to understand what she did, from her perspective."

"What's to understand?" He kept one hand firmly on her wrist, put his other arm around her waist and started walking again. "She disobeyed her father's wishes, shamed her family and village, dishonored the man she was promised to, and put her own future in serious jeopardy."

She shook free of his hold, pushing him away. "You are truly unbelievable."

"Why the hell does it matter, anyway? It has nothing to do with us."

"Doesn't it?"

"No. Damn it, woman. Who are you and what have you done with the sweet thing I kissed earlier?"

She stalked down the path and retorted, "She didn't realize you were so cynical about love."

Whoa. *That's* what this was about?

"You planning on falling in love with me, Zoë?" he called after her.

She came to an abrupt halt. "No! Of course not."

"Then what's the problem?"

When he caught up to her she was standing in a small patch of moonlight. Her blond hair and bare shoulders shimmered in the heat like liquid gold and silver. He couldn't decipher the look on her face. But it wasn't happy.

"No problem," she said, baring her teeth in a smile so forced it made *his* teeth hurt. "No problem at all." She spun to continue walking.

He snagged her arm and spun her back. Now he was getting angry.

"Look. We already agreed we don't want to get involved, right? I told you I was a mess and I meant it. My ex-wife screwed me so bad it's taken five years to dig myself out of the hole, both financially and emotionally. So, yeah. Forgive me if I'm a little cynical about love."

He heard her swallow. He tugged her hard, so she mashed into his chest. "But I didn't think we were talking about love here, Zoë. I thought we were talking about something else entirely."

She sucked in a sharp breath and for a nanosecond he was sure she would slap him. Instead her nipples went hard. He felt them all the way through the silk of her dress and the cotton of his shirt. Instantly *he* went hard.

This was more like it.

He swooped down and kissed her. But this time it wasn't a soft exploration or a tentative kiss of seduction as he'd given her before. This time it was rough and needy and uncivilized. *Just like him.*

He used his hands. He pulled her tight into him so she could feel his need, then swept them up her body to her breasts, capturing the tips between his fingers. He squeezed, groaning at the feel of her soft, firm flesh against his palms and the squirm of her body as it reacted to the pleasure.

She gasped. He pressed into her in the near-complete darkness. "Yeah. *That's* what I'm talkin' about."

A second later she did slap him. Then turned and stalked away.

"Zoë!" he snapped. "Be care—"

But it was too late. She shrieked and he heard her go down hard on the ground.

"God *damn* it!" He let fly a few more choice swear words and in two strides he'd reached her, crouching down. "Are you hurt?"

Muddy hands collided with his as she tried to bat at him. "Go away! I'm fine!"

"Enough!" he growled, and swept her up into his arms, mud and all. He threw her unceremoniously over his shoulder. "Now we do it my way."

Chapter 5

"Oof!"

Something hard and unyielding punched Zoë in the stomach. She couldn't get her bearings. She was being jostled, her head was whirling like helicopter blades and she actually felt as if she was upside down.

Struggling, she grappled for purchase and her palms met solid muscle. "Ouch!" Her hands were also full of grit and scrapes and hurt like heck. Her knees throbbed and stung every time she banged them into…something equally hard and unyielding.

"Stop squirming or you'll break both our necks," a furious male voice growled.

Breeze.

Breeze, who had just kissed her. And copped a feel. A really good feel. The memory blazed past the stars bursting in her head like the *Millennium Falcon* going into hyperspace. My God! He was *still* copping a feel! Except now his hand was firmly latched onto her backside. And he was carrying her over his *shoulder!*

"Put me down!" she demanded, pounding at him despite the stinging in her hands.

He grunted like a caveman—how appropriate!—but continued lumbering through the dark, humid jungle at what from her crazy angle seemed to be breakneck speed.

"And get your hands off my ass!" she added in her most authoritative tone. Hard to be authoritative when you were dangling over someone's shoulder like a sack of potatoes. Or a captive from the next cave down…

His fingers gripped her derrière tighter. To her dismay she realized her dress had ridden completely up. And *naturally* she'd decided to wear a thong today.

She also noted that the masculine hand on her almost-bare bottom was large and strong. Calluses peppered his palms and the pads of his fingers. The muscles bulging in the shoulder and biceps that carried her were ripped and corded. And the bit of male anatomy under the cargo shorts she clung to was smooth, lean and firm.

Oh. My. God.

It had to be the blood rushing to her upside-down head, but…she was actually getting turned on.

She groaned in self-disgust.

She felt him glance back at her. "You all right back there?"

"What do you think?" she muttered.

His fingers squeezed. "Feel fine to me."

"I am *so* hating you right now."

"Yeah, whatever. We're almost to the beach. I'll let you down there—"

"*Ha*-ting you."

"—where there's no risk of you breaking your neck."

"No, it's gonna be yours."

He chuckled darkly. "We'll see who breaks first." His large, strong hand impudently caressed her butt.

She snapped her mouth shut on her next retort. The man was truly insufferable. Which was why it was so mortifying that her body was reacting the way it was to his touch and his arrogant male certainty that she would end up in his bed tonight.

Reacting with excitement.

True to his word, a few long strides later they broke free of the jungle, and he stopped on the beach to swing her down from his shoulder and set her uncertain feet on the sand. Somewhere along the way she'd lost her flip-flops.

He kept his arms around her until she regained her balance, then leaned down, obviously intending to kiss her.

She jumped back and held her hands up. "No way. This is so not happening."

He tipped his handsome head in the moonlight and regarded her. The very corner of his lips curved up with some sentiment she couldn't decipher. Amusement? Calculation? Frustration?

Possibly all of the above.

"Right," he said with another negligent lift of the shoulder, which then morphed into a formal bow. He swept his hand toward the trail back to the Indigo Inn. "After you."

Better. "Thank you."

She started walking, sticking to the sandy path. It was the long stretch of beach punctuated by tide pools. Sparkling and winking like pots of dark jewels every time a wave came in, the pools overflowed onto the surrounding black rocks, then slowly emptied to the sound of a thousand splashing fountains. It was magical.

"Your head okay?" Breeze asked, bringing her back to reality.

"It's good," she said. She hadn't really hit it in the fall. She'd just been disoriented from being upside down. Her hands and knees had taken the brunt. And her dress, which was hopelessly stained by the mud. Two designer dresses ruined in one day. Had to be a record.

"The rest of you seems fine," he observed.

She wasn't fooled by his casual tone. She could feel his eyes on her…hot, intense, interested. On her back and shoulders. Her legs. And her derrière. Especially that. She tried not to let herself sway as she walked. But that only made her more self-conscious. It made her think about his hands on it. On all of her. It made her *want* his hands on all of her.

Oh, God.

She ground her teeth and withstood the rising tension all the way to the end of the tide pools, where the rocky shore gave way to a small sheltered lagoon. By then she felt like she was walking along naked.

Abruptly, she whipped around. "Stop it!"

He halted a few feet away, hands on hips. "What?"

"Stop looking at me like that."

"Like what?"

"Like…" She clenched her jaw.

"Like I want to have sex with you?" he helpfully supplied.

"Yes!" she burst out. "Like that!"

"Sorry. No can do."

"Excuse me?"

"Because I *do* want to have sex with you, Zoë." He took a step closer to her. "And what's more, you want to have sex with me." Before she could voice an objection, he said, "Hell, woman, we've got enough chemistry to wake up that ol' dormant volcano. And when we finally do have sex, I'll wager the whole island will shake from the fireworks." He took another step, leaning in toward her. "So, no. I won't stop looking at you like that."

She mirrored his stance, hands fisted on her hips, and leaned in, too. "Fine. Go ahead and look all you like. Just know that it's not—"

"It *is* gonna happen, sweet thing," he interrupted. "That I can guarantee."

Her jaw dropped and she stared at him, speechless. Of all the arrogant, maddening, chauvinist…

But he just straightened, glanced out at the ocean, then back at her, and grinned. "Meanwhile, let's go for a swim."

But she was still trying to wrap her brain around his bald it's-gonna-happen statement.

The worst part? She believed him.

She scrambled to shore up her defenses. "Are you out of your mind?"

"Hell, no. The water's great here," he said, no doubt deliberately misunderstanding her. He pulled his shirt over his head and tossed it next to the bag he'd dropped on the sand. "Hardly any waves and just deep enough to touch bottom. Nice and warm, too, this time of year."

Maybe if she ignored the whole previous subject, it would go away.

"Who swims at night, anyhow?" she muttered, gazing out at the waves gently lapping at the pristine sand beach. The moon was just bright enough to paint the sand a luminous white and chase away the inky blackness of the sea, teasing a deep shade of Fiji's signature turquoise from its depths. She hated to admit, it did look inviting.

"I do, all the time," he said. "It's better at night." He winked, and reached for the waistband of his shorts. "The sharks are all asleep."

"Except the two-legged variety," she mumbled, her alarm growing exponentially as he pulled down his zipper. "We don't have bathing suits with us," she pointed out in case he'd forgotten.

"So? It's not like you haven't seen me naked before," he said oh-so-reasonably. "Or I, you."

He stripped out of his pants, dropped them and ran into the water, splashing through the waves with a whoop. At least she assumed he did, because she'd squeezed her eyes shut at the first flash of— Well, never mind what he was flashing.

"I am *not* going skinny-dipping with you, Breeze!" she called. Absolutely not.

"Open your eyes, Zoë," he called back from several yards out. "What are you so afraid of?"

She started to answer, but the words stuck in her throat.

Good question. What *was* she afraid of?

Losing her job? Losing her mind? Surely not losing this chance with him?

She opened her eyes and saw him standing there with waves slapping at his muscular thighs, watching her, and she suddenly knew none of those things mattered nearly as much as the one thing she had never even considered before this very moment.

Losing her heart.

Despite her annoyance with the infuriating man, she already had a hell of a crush on him. What would it do to her to let him make love to her, and then be forced to leave him at the end of the week?

But what would it do to her to leave at the end of the week and *not* have made love to this amazingly tempting man…?

Oh, lord. She was going to do it, wasn't she? She was going to let him make love to her and damn the consequences.

She watched as he let himself fall gracefully onto his back in the water, floating there in the gentle waves, beckoning her with his dark, sinful eyes. "C'mon. Think of those amazing kisses. You know you want more. You know you want *me*."

This just wasn't fair. His gloriously naked body was bathed in the silver moonlight, making him stand out against the dark, rippling water like some incredibly sensual sea god. His growing arousal stood out, too, silently taunting her. Okay, *tempting* her.

"I'm furious with you, you know," she called in a last-ditch effort to turn the tide of what was happening.

"Nah. You're just mad because I'm right."

Unfortunate but true.

He waggled his eyebrows and teased her, "C'mon. Sex on the beach with the mysterious owner of the bed-and-breakfast…"

The image literally made a shiver run through her whole body. "The mysterious gardener, you mean," she grumbled. But she was already reaching for the button of her halter.

What was she doing?

Her dress dropped to the wet sand around her ankles.

Smiling in triumph, he wiggled his fingers at her like a demon luring a little girl. "I'll be anybody you want me to be, sweet thing. I'll make all your fantasies come true."

Sealing her fate, that's what.

It was ridiculous the rush of excitement Sean felt as Zoë walked slowly through the waves toward him. There was something primitive, primal, about watching a naked woman come to him for the first time, knowing he would soon be buried deep in her body. Especially when she came to him so damned reluctantly. Like she desperately didn't want to, but couldn't help herself because his sexual allure was too great. It was enough to inflate a man's ego. And a few other things, besides.

He was so hard it should be painful. But it felt good. Really good. And so did she when she finally reached him and floated into his waiting arms. Her body was smooth and warm as he crushed it against his; her mouth was hot and opened readily for his kiss. He felt a tremble run through her, and experienced a jolt of masculine gratification like he'd never felt before in his life.

Acting on pure, feral instinct, he lifted her by her thighs and in a single, urgent motion impaled her on his impatient arousal.

She cried out in surprise. He was pretty shocked himself. What was it about this woman that turned him into a caveman?

But that uncomfortable thought didn't stop him from adjusting her legs around his waist and thrusting in even deeper. She moaned, clung to him and wrapped her arms around his neck.

"Sorry. Couldn't wait," he croaked past the heart thundering in his throat and the breath backed up in his lungs. "Couldn't chance you'd change your mind."

"As if." She wriggled down the last few millimeters of his cock and he groaned in pleasure.

"Breeze," she said abruptly in a strangled whisper, pulling back to look at him.

"Yeah, babe?"

"I'm not on the pill."

He swallowed. Okay. A complication, but only in terms of timing. He took a very deep breath to steady himself. "Right. Give me a minute."

"I'm sorry."

"Don't be." In truth, hearing that detail about her stroked his male ego—again—in a completely irrational way. It confirmed that being with him was special to her. That *he* was special to her. Very special.

Which really should make him run screaming in the other direction. After all, the last thing he wanted was a woman thinking he was special, or any kind of relationship material. So why didn't he run?

Possibly, being inside her was clouding his judgment. At the moment he didn't care.

"We just have to make it back as far as my shorts pocket." She might not have come prepared, but he sure as hell had. Too bad he didn't want to let her go that long.

"You brought protection?" She sounded taken aback.

"Damn straight."

He covered her mouth and kissed her deep and hard, so she'd know with certainty that this was no accident. He'd meant her to be right where she was. Even if he'd been in denial himself for a while.

She felt so incredibly good, so hot and wet and tight gloved around him, no way did he want to stop now. But he was afraid if he kept kissing her and she kept kissing him back, in no time he wouldn't have the willpower.

He pulled out and they both gasped, panting from frustrated excitement. Or was it loss? For a second she clung tighter, then her legs loosened and slid down his hips. He grabbed her before she could get away completely. She'd been just skittish enough all night that he didn't want her second-guessing her decision to be with him.

"You're my lover now," he murmured low in her ear. "I've been in your body and I'm coming back for more."

She reached up and kissed him, reassuring him with her sultry hum of anticipation that she wanted him just as much as he wanted her.

And the sooner the better. He banded his arms around her waist and picked her up, wading toward shore as their mouths and bodies melded in delicious heat. She was perfect. Her curves fit his hollows as if they were made for each other. He felt her toes curl against his legs; the hard peaks of her breasts poked impatiently into his chest.

"I want you," she whispered. "Now."

How was he supposed to resist such a plea? He'd made it to where the ocean waves reached out with wide, sinuous fingers to caress the sand—but still a good ten feet from his shorts.

Screw it.

With a growl, he dropped to his knees, landing between her thighs, and covered her with his body. *Damn*, he wanted to *own* her, every inch of her! He kissed her for all he was worth, holding her tight and rolling her through the surf when she met him kiss for kiss, touch for touch, dueling with him for dominance in their fevered quest for possession of each other. Over and over and over they rolled, back and forth, until he was dizzy from the need and want of her.

He needed more.

Dragging her up above the waterline, he slid down between her thighs, spread them wide and took her with his mouth. She cried out and her body bowed as he ravished her with his tongue, reveling in the taste of her passion. Almost instantly she cried out again and her body convulsed, bucking with the unrelenting pleasure he pressed upon her, not letting up even when she moaned and writhed and begged him to stop or surely she would shatter in a million pieces. He didn't stop. Not until she did shatter. Utterly, completely. Sobbing out his nickname over and over.

She would be his. *She belonged to him.*

Almost.

He lifted his head to get his bearings and saw his shorts were within reach. *There was a God.*

Ten seconds later he plunged into her with the guttural roar of a conquest denied far too long. Which was absurd. He'd known the woman less than twelve hours. But that didn't make his need for her any less fierce. He was fist-thick and steel-hard from the taste of her on his tongue and the sound of his name echoing in the night.

He scythed deep and sure. Her breath sucked in and her voice cracked on another cry. Her blue eyes were wild and wide as she looked up at him, like she was poised on the brink of desperation. Then her body splintered yet again.

This time it was too much for him. His own sex exploded in a climax that ripped through his body like a tidal wave, battering his senses, crashing through his will with a pleasure so profound he was left prostrate and gasping for breath on top of her when it finally subsided to a low, throbbing aftermath.

Under him, she swore softly. "Whoa."

"Yeah," he said, his head spinning. "That was a little unexpected."

She actually sounded afraid. Of the intensity of what had just happened? Or of what might happen next…?

She wasn't the only one confused. A million conflicting emotions speared through him when she whispered threadily, "What do we do now?"

He raised up on his elbows and gazed down at her. And went with the obvious.

"Now we go back to my place and do it all over again."

Chapter 6

The sun was just about to peek over the horizon when Sean woke to the familiar sound of a boat motor slowly chugging through the predawn silence. Someone was here early, he thought muzzily, and rolled over to snuggle against the curve of Zoë's warm, naked body. Memories of last night's lovemaking brought a big smile to his face. Damn, the woman was hot.

They'd finally run back to the boathouse in desperation after using up all three of the just-in-case condoms he'd brought with him last night making love on the beach. They'd dispensed with a few more once they'd made it as far as his bedroom overlooking Indigo Bay. His smile widened. Last night she'd said the view there was stimulating. Inspirational even. Oh, yeah, and the view out the window was pretty nice, too.

He'd let her be on top. The least he could do after those kind of props.

Speaking of props, the distant sound of the boat's motor was getting louder. In fact, it seemed to be pulling in at the Indigo's dock. Sounded like a big craft. Probably some lost tourist yacht looking for fuel and a meal. Damn. He did not want to move from this bed. But his working staff wasn't reporting in for three more days, including the kid he'd hired as his marine attendant. Sean's living quarters were upstairs, but downstairs the boathouse was the real deal, gas pump and all.

Outside the bedroom window a familiar flapping of red-and-green wings accompanied a pair of high-pitched dogs barking. Scarlett and Rhett playing burglar alarm. Well, at least they weren't playing at tigers and bears this morning, or worse. Their repertoire of animal imitations was fairly formidable, but could be a bit much before one's first cup of coffee.

He gave a sigh as he heard the sound of men's voices and heavy footsteps coming down the wooden jetty. Real people, not parrots. Any second now they'd be ringing the ship's bell that hung by the door with its small sign, Ring for Service.

May as well grab his pants and try to head them off before the clanging woke Zoë. He lightly kissed her hair, reluctantly let her go and started to slide out of bed.

"Where you goin'?" she murmured, her sleepy eyes fluttering open as she rolled to catch him. She looked so damned delectable lying there in his bed, her golden hair flung every which way on his pillow, the rosy blush on her cheeks evidence of his loving.

"Early customers," he said, leaning back in for a lingering morning kiss. "Go back to sleep. I'll just be a few minutes."

"Are you the *only* employee in this place?" she complained, pushing out her lower lip. God, she was sweet.

He chuckled. "You might say that. At the moment, anyway. Other than Aruna, of course."

She harrumphed. "Your boss is a slave driver. I'll have to have a word with Mr. Guthrie about this situation."

He grinned. "Yeah. You definitely will," he said, and planted a kiss on the end of her nose. "When I get back we need to talk."

"I can think of better ways to spend our time."

She looked at him coyly from under her lashes and he forgot his name, along with everything else going on, except finding out exactly what better ways she meant. He reached for her greedily. It was only the sudden loud clanging from the ship's bell downstairs that jerked him out of the spell she wove around him whenever her naked skin touched his.

He let out a rough curse.

"Don't move," he said impatiently.

Then he swiped up a pair of white drawstring pants hanging out of his top dresser drawer and jammed his legs into them as he hurried down the stairs two at a time. Approaching the door, he glanced out the back window. There was a police boat tied up at the dock.

Excellent. Maybe they'd found his damn yacht.

Behind him, he heard a series of creaks at the top of the stairs. Reaching for the doorknob, he turned to see Zoë standing with a hand on the newel post wearing an adoring smile and not much more. His eyes widened, and he shot her an exasperated half grin and half frown. She'd wrapped the sheet around herself but was obviously nude under it. And what they'd been doing all night was written all over her face.

Outside, someone pounded rudely on the door and shouted, "Sean Guthrie!"

"Yeah, yeah," he called back, shooing her with a hand so she'd go back in the bedroom, out of sight. If she didn't, they'd be the talk of several islands within minutes, for sure.

But for some reason her jaw dropped and a puzzled look spread over her face. She didn't budge.

The guy knocked again even louder, and yelled, "Open the door, Guthrie! We know you're in there."

Oh, for God's sake. He flung open the door. *"What?"*

He was greeted by three burly Fijian cops. One cop was holding an official-looking piece of paper, the second cop a pair of handcuffs and the third had his hand resting on a nasty-looking sidearm.

"Are you Sean Guthrie?" the guy with the paper asked.

He nodded. "Yeah?"

"Please step outside, sir, and put your hands behind your back."

"Ex*cuse* me? What's this all about?"

"Sean Guthrie, you are under arrest for murder."

Chapter 7

Stunned didn't even come close. Zoë simply could not believe what she was seeing and hearing.

The man she'd spent the night with—under—was *Sean Guthrie*? Not some random beach bum gardener named Breeze, but Sean Guthrie? Owner of the Indigo Inn and frat buddy to her boss—*that* Sean Guthrie?

And he'd just been arrested for murder?

Murder!

The metallic snicking of handcuffs being tightened brought her abruptly back to the present.

"Hey! Excuse me!" she yelled as the three Fijian cops pushed Breeze...er, *Sean Guthrie* through the door. She ran down the stairs clutching the sheet to her body with one hand and hanging on to the banister with the other so she wouldn't trip. "This has to be a mistake!"

He couldn't be a murderer! She'd *slept* with the man.

"Of course it's a freaking mistake," Breeze—that is, Sean—said with a jerk at his metal bonds. "Completely ludicrous charge. Who the hell am I supposed to have killed?"

She couldn't decide if she felt more duped, incredulous or just plain angry with him. Oddly, she didn't feel terrified, which was what any sensible woman would be feeling when confronted by the fact that she'd willingly given her body to a killer.

"First a dead guy, now a murderer," she muttered. "Never a dull moment around you."

He actually looked affronted. "Only after *you* showed up."

The cop holding the paper came to attention. "What dead guy?"

Except Sean Guthrie *wasn't* a killer. Just a charming liar. He must have guessed that she was his Secret Traveler. Had he really thought he could seduce her to get a good rating?

"There's no dead guy," her duplicitous lover said through gritted teeth, giving her the evil eye. "I was tired and passed out in the hammock. *She* thought I was dead. Obviously I'm not."

The three cops looked from him to her and back again. "You might as well confess," Handcuffs Cop told him. "If there are more bodies we'll find them." His eyes strayed to *her* body. She tightened her hold on the sheet.

"I did *not* kill anyone!" Breeze enunciated. "Who—?"

She took a deep breath and interrupted, "It couldn't

have been him. I was with Breeze…Sean…this *man* all night." Whatever his name and his game were, he hadn't left her sight all night. Handcuffs Cop grinned broadly.

Paper Cop gave her a look that said he didn't give a damn. "If you wish to make a statement, you can follow us over to the police station in Savusavu."

With that, Sidearm Cop gave Breeze a none-too-gentle push down the steps to the dock and the police bay cruiser.

"Zoë, ask Aruna if she'll take care of things until I get this mess straightened out," Breeze—*Sean* called over his shoulder. "And we still need to talk!"

You think?

A chaos of emotions bombarded Zoë as they marched her lover away. He looked tired again. When his eyes sought hers one last time, they looked a million years old. But his tanned shoulders and back—they hadn't even let him put on a shirt—were straight and proud. No sign of guilt in his steady stride. Not that she'd for a second believed he was a killer. He might be a scoundrel and a manipulator, but the man who'd made love to her all night could never have harmed another human being. Even in their wildest abandon, his touch had been sensitive, his attentions selfless. Last night his pleasure had been all about hers.

Okay, so he had an agenda, but a murderer? No way.

Still, what could she do to help him? She didn't know a soul in Fiji other than him and Aruna. The American embassy was hundreds of miles away on another island. Maybe she should call them. On the other hand, Sean Guthrie was a big boy and clearly had been around the block a time or two. Maybe he wouldn't even want her help.

The big blue-and-white cruiser backed away from the dock, turned and took off at a fast clip, leaving a rooster tail of white spray in its wake. The sun was up now, casting a pale golden glow over the deep turquoise water of the bay, and popping the stands of waving palms along the shore into bright green relief against the darker jungle behind.

Well, too bad if he didn't want her help. She really did have to think of something. *Do* something. Because if the owner of the Indigo Inn was in jail, she couldn't give the place its five-star rating. I mean, jeez, what traveler would want to stay in a remote island hideaway run by an accused murderer? And felon or not, if she didn't give the boss's good friend a stellar rating, she might as well kiss *adios* to her career plans at the Secret Traveler. Circumstances wouldn't matter; Sean Guthrie was the boss's frat brother. Plus, if she gave the inn a low rating, Sean would possibly be furious enough to tell her boss they'd slept together. Wouldn't *that* be just dandy.

Objective? Professional? Try unemployed.

Not good. Something must be done.

She'd ask Aruna for advice. That's what she'd do. Maybe between them they could figure out how to get Sean out of jail and her out of this mess.

Then she could give him his darn rating and get the heck out of Dodge before anything else happened. Because it surely would. One thing he was exactly right about. Ever since she'd arrived at the Indigo Inn, she'd landed herself in one disaster after another.

Good grief. Dead guys. Killers. Sex on the beach.

Hello? Succumbing to the temptation of the inn's sexy owner had been the biggest disaster of all. What on earth had she been thinking?

Unfortunately, *thinking* was the last thing on her mind whenever he started to kiss her. A mistake she wouldn't let happen again.

Even if the rogue had given her the most incredible night of her life.

Maybe she should call Alicia and Madeline. Ask their advice. Maybe they were going through similar adventures at the resorts they were evaluating.

Yeah. Right.

Letting loose a heartfelt groan, she headed for the bedroom to get dressed and go find Aruna.

Like she'd said, a pure disaster.

"Regi Akilu," Aruna pronounced with a firm nod. "He's the one we need. Right away. Come."

Aruna headed out of the inn's kitchen so fast Zoë had to run to catch up. She barely had time to grab her purse and the bag with a shirt she'd collected for Breeze. Sean.

"Who's Regi Akilu?" she asked as she followed Aruna down the beach path that held far too many vivid memories of the man they were trying to save from jail.

"Regi is a very good lawyer. He spends most of his time away on Vanua Levu, but his home is here in the village. He will help Mr. Breeze."

Which brought up another nagging question. "Why doesn't anyone call him Mr. Guthrie? I can't believe I thought he was the gardener."

"He is the gardener. And the carpenter. The mechanic.

And everything else that needs doing around here." Aruna gave her a sideways glance. "He doesn't like being called Mr. Guthrie. Says he left Mr. Guthrie back with his old life in the States, that now he is free as the breeze." She shrugged. "But he is my boss, so I call him *Mr.* Breeze."

Free as the breeze. So, Zoë's first instinct had been right on target.

Not that it mattered. *She* was free as the breeze, too, with no plans to change. The only ties she wanted right now were to her job.

But maybe her second instinct, the one where he had concealed his identity from her on purpose, maybe that wasn't true. She hoped it wasn't. She'd have to ask him about it when she saw him.

Or maybe not. Because in the end, that didn't really matter, either. Whatever his motives, his inn's rating would not be affected by her sleeping with him. So it didn't really matter who he was.

But it *did* matter if he was in jail.

Luckily, she and Aruna caught Regi Akilu eating breakfast with friends and family before departing for the big island. She immediately recognized him as the man wearing the colorful shirt who had officiated at the opening *yaqona* ceremony last night.

"*Bula, bula!*" he greeted them, rising with the ubiquitous Fijian salutation, then launched into praise of Aruna's dancing from last night. A cheerful, smiling man, his gray hair and graceful demeanor lent him an air of dignity that inspired confidence. Zoë listened anxiously as Aruna interrupted his compliments and animatedly informed him of her boss's arrest.

Immediately, Mr. Akilu became serious. He asked

Zoë a dozen specific questions about the police and exactly what they'd done and said that morning. Then he said, "Give me a moment," disappeared and a few minutes later reappeared with his briefcase in hand and said to Zoë, "Let's go. We'll take my scooter."

"Where?" She matched his fast clip around the back of the beautifully woven and thatched house. "What about Aruna?" she asked when the other woman didn't come with them.

"Only room for one passenger."

The scooter turned out to be an antique Vespa that puttered and coughed its way to the ferry landing located two miles away on the other side of the narrow island. The ride down the volcano was bone-rattling but it got them there faster than walking. When they arrived at the dock, he simply left the Vespa leaning against a tree.

"Won't it be stolen?" she asked.

"On the island we share everything," he said with a proud smile. "No such thing as stealing here. When I need it, it will be returned."

She tried to imagine such a thing happening in Chicago, and shook her head. "What a nice way to live. I envy you."

At the wide quay he hailed a man loading passengers into a large speedboat and he and Zoë squished onto its aft bench along with a chattering family of five. "The ferry runs only once a day," he explained as they gingerly put their feet on a pile of luggage. "But we're in luck because a lot of people came for the celebration last night and are leaving now."

By the end of the two-hour boat ride to Savusavu she

was great friends with them all, had been well fed on leftovers from the feast and was feeling numb again from two bowls of *yaqona*, which apparently Fijians drank all the time, not just at celebrations.

No wonder they were all so friendly here.

Long before they tied up at the busy marina, she'd already forgiven Breeze, or Sean, or whatever the heck his name was, and was actually looking forward to seeing him again.

The family in the speedboat had been horrified when they heard of his arrest and regaled her with stories of his kindness and generosity, even when he'd been so poor he was living in an abandoned hut on the outskirts of the village. That was around the time he'd bartered his extensive American CD collection for a broken-down, derelict fishing boat, which he'd taken the winter to fix and restore while getting to know the entire Taveuni Island group by going out with the village fishermen to lend a hand. Then he'd started hiring himself out to the droves of eco-tourists that flocked to see the natural wonders of their country. He'd made enough money that first season to buy two clunker boats the next winter, and even though the family made it clear that Fijians in general disapprove of conspicuous acquisitiveness, Mr. Breeze never flaunted his material success, but rather, shared the rewards generously with his neighbors as befitted a wise and great man. The villagers all adored him.

By the time Zoë and Regi Akilu walked into the small, provincial police station in Savusavu, she was having a hard time remembering why she shouldn't adore him, too. She certainly had last night.

Wait. That's right. He'd lied to her.

Or had he?

She was so confused. She really had to lay off that *yaqona* stuff.

At the front desk of the police station, Mr. Akilu announced he was Sean Guthrie's attorney, and demanded to see his client. Zoë kept her mouth shut, her eyes open and watched in awe as he worked his lawyer magic on the irritated detective inspector who had been sent from the capital city to assist the local cops, who in turn appeared more accustomed to riding herd on drunken tourists than investigating real crime—in their defense, mainly because there didn't seem to be any.

But the crime Breeze was accused of was a doozie. Sitting in the cramped waiting room she heard much of the story through the thin walls of the station. Apparently, the American couple, the Blantons, whom Breeze had argued with two nights ago about his missing yacht had been brutally murdered mere hours later. Stabbed repeatedly as the pair had made love on the beach. A shiver went all the way down her spine when she heard that part. Talk about a creepy coincidence.

It also explained why the police hadn't cared that Zoë spent last night with him. The killings had happened night *before* last.

The good news was that the arresting officers had never formally booked him, for lack of evidence. In fact, he had supplied the names of a dozen witnesses who could place him on his boat in the local marina at the time of the Blanton murders. So after allowing them to question Breeze for three grueling hours—asking the same pointless questions over and over—Mr. Akilu finally told them in no uncertain terms what he'd do if they didn't either arrest or release his client immediately.

Five hours after arriving at the police station, Sean Guthrie walked out into the bright Fijian afternoon sunshine to where Zoë was waiting out front.

She gave him a smile of profound relief and joy.

Too bad he didn't share her warm, fuzzy feelings. The moment he saw her he came to an abrupt halt and stared, looking distinctly unhappy.

"Zoë? What the hell are *you* doing here?"

Sean was astonished to see Zoë standing on the sidewalk expectantly when he emerged from the police station ahead of his good friend and rescuer, Regi Akilu.

What a disaster! Bad enough to be hauled in by the cops and accused of murder in front of his new lover—the one he should never have slept with in the first place, for so many reasons it made his head spin. And now here she was. Holding his humiliation over his spinning head and his fate in her all-too-talented hands.

Her chin lifted. "I thought you might want to get out of jail," she said defensively, her pretty blue eyes clouding over with hurt.

He ignored the spike of guilt that poked at him. "I did. I just didn't expect you to help." If anything, the opposite.

"You thought maybe I'd just go back to bed?" she asked, incredulous.

He shook his head, trying not to think of the five-star rating he needed so badly, and his rapidly tanking chances of getting it. "I guess I assumed Aruna arranged for Regi to come."

"Well, if it's any consolation, she did." But from the look on Zoë's face he knew his assumptions had been all wrong. Before he could say anything, she handed him a plastic bag. "Anyway, I didn't know if they'd give you a shirt, so I brought one."

Touched despite his knee-jerk misgivings, he accepted it and slipped it on gratefully. "Thanks."

The woman was full of surprises. She'd bailed him out *and* brought clothes. After they'd dragged him away from her bed in handcuffs. For murder.

He tried to remember the last time a woman he was involved with had gone out of her way to help him— no, not cook a meal or pick up movie tickets, but really *help* him. He drew a blank. No one ever had. Before Zoë.

It felt nice. Surprisingly nice.

Too nice.

What was in it for her?

"Why are you doing this?" he asked her after Regi had come out of the station with his paperwork, pumped Sean's hand and clapped him on the back with an admonition to stay out of trouble and call him if the cops hassled him again. Regi hurried off down the street.

"Someone had to. You're innocent." But her smile was brittle and stopped well shy of her defensive eyes. His fault.

"You're sure about that?"

She blinked. "Are you saying you're not?"

"Of course I am. Innocent. I just…" He took a breath and a mental step back. *Not everyone was like his ex-*

wife, he reminded himself. Zoë seemed genuinely concerned. *For* him, not about him. "I'm just surprised. You barely know me. But thank you," he said sincerely.

She crossed her arms over her abdomen, looking everywhere but at him. "You're welcome."

Yeah, clearly he'd blown it. In record time he'd managed to alienate her completely and destroy the incredible closeness they'd shared last night. God, he was such a cynical bastard.

"Zoë…" He reached for her, contrite. "I'm sorry. I've been a real jerk."

She put up her hands in a defensive gesture. "No, you're right. My reasons for helping were strictly professional."

He supposed he deserved that—*and* to have his worst fears confirmed. When he didn't question her statement, she said, "I suppose you guessed I'm you're Secret Traveler."

"I had my suspicions."

"Then you know I couldn't give the Indigo Inn the rating it deserves with you in jail accused of murder."

He knew. But one thing did catch him unprepared. "You're finished with the evaluation already?"

"Pretty much."

"But the full staff hasn't even arrived yet," he protested. If she was done, he had no hope of repairing this morning's damage. Or last night's. "How can your rating be complete without the full picture of the amenities provided by staff?" he argued.

She cleared her throat. "Under the circumstances, I think it's best I leave as soon as—"

"No," he said, shaking his head firmly. "It wouldn't be fair to—" Suddenly, a thought struck him square between the eyes. He narrowed them. "What circumstances? Surely, you don't think I had sex with you last night to get a better guidebook rating?"

She studied her strappy sandal as she dug the toe into a crack in the pavement. "Wouldn't be the first time it's happened." Then her face went crimson and she quickly looked up. "Not to me, of course. I would never—" Flustered, she halted in midsentence and pressed her lips together. A few seconds went by. "Did you?"

God, he would *not* be offended.

"Us sleeping together had nothing to do with your job," he assured her, fighting a growing anger. Anger with her or himself, he wasn't quite sure. This was all so screwed-up he couldn't think straight. "At least on my part. I'd have hoped you felt that without being told."

He grasped her arm and started walking. The front entry of the police station was not the place for this conversation.

"Where are we going?"

"To the marina. I'm putting you on a boat back to the Indigo."

She went along without protest, but he didn't let go of her arm. Not that he expected her to run away. But for some perverse reason he needed the contact with her. Needed to touch her warm flesh, even if she didn't want to touch him back. Not that he blamed her.

Neither of them spoke for a block or two. Then she said, "Why didn't you tell me who you really are, Sean?"

He'd been wondering when that would come up. "I tried."

"When?" she asked accusingly.

"Every time you called me the damned gardener. But somehow I always got interrupted."

A small frown appeared between her brows. But she didn't argue. "Okay," she finally said. Miracles.

"You believe me?"

"Yes."

"And that I didn't try to manipulate you with great sex?"

She gave a nod, but looked embarrassed about that part. "I didn't really think that. I just…"

"Just…?"

"Don't have a lot of experience with this sort of thing. I was hoping I hadn't made a huge mistake in judgment."

Something compelled him to ask, "And did you?"

For the first time she squarely met his gaze. "Apparently."

"No," he said with a sigh. "No, you didn't. You just had the bad luck to exercise your good judgment with a total bastard. A bastard who couldn't be sorrier."

He halted and tugged her close, wrapping his hand around her jaw. He kissed her, and whispered into her mouth, "If I promise to be better, I hope you'll continue to exercise that good judgment for the rest of your stay."

She pulled back. "Sean, I really do think it's better if I leave and go on to my next—"

"No." He kissed her again.

"But I honestly—"

"No." He felt her weaken. So he kissed her again, and again, until he felt her muscles go pliant and willing.

"But—"

"I'm not ready to let you go yet, Zoë. Now that both our cards are on the table there's no reason you can't stay and finish your evaluation of the staff's effectiveness. Just a few more days." He couldn't resist adding in a low whisper, "I swear I'll make it worth your while."

"Now you really are trying to bribe me."

Maybe if she hadn't sounded so damn hopeful he would have denied it. But her tantalizing sex-kitten purr had him instantly hard and thinking about everything they'd done last night, and even more, what they hadn't gotten around to doing yet.

"Who, me?" he murmured. Damn, he couldn't wait to get started. "Nah. I swear I'm innocent."

Chapter 8

"Doesn't it worry you that the police think you're a murderer?" Zoë asked Sean when they were seated at his favorite table on the outside deck at the Savusavu Yacht Club. They hadn't found her a ride back to the Indigo yet, and he hadn't eaten since last night, so he was starving. Zoë was sipping a fresh papaya daiquiri, looking at him with a concerned frown.

"They let me go, didn't they?" He took a mouthful of delicious fish chowder and washed it down with a slug of Fiji Gold. Heaven.

"Not without a fight, Sean. It's obvious the cops think you're guilty."

He set down his beer. "I did not kill the Blantons! And I have plenty of witnesses that put me elsewhere. The cops have no case."

"Yeah, but that detective inspector kept talking about motive. Your missing yacht has to be worth a lot of money. Which makes a damn good motive."

That detective inspector, Sergeant Ram Sanjit, had shot his mouth about a lot of things. A royal pain in the ass, that guy.

"It's just a boat. And it's insured. Certainly not worth killing over."

"Tell that to the inspector."

"I did. About a hundred times. I think it finally sank in."

Her brow beetled. "He seemed pretty determined to me."

"More like lazy. If I'm guilty he doesn't have to hunt the real killer. Look, can we talk about something else?"

"We should do it."

"That's more like—"

"Hunt the real killer, I mean."

He froze with his beer halfway to his lips. "Are you nuts? Why would we do that?"

She drummed her fingers on the teak tabletop. "If we don't, Sanjit will find a way to put you in jail. I know he will."

Sean tipped his head, not sure what to say. Or how to feel about her obvious interest in his well-being. He appreciated her concern. He did. But he didn't want her getting the idea they were in this together. Or in *anything* together, for that matter, other than bed. They'd been through all that.

She kept drumming. "Obviously the murders and the missing yacht are somehow connected."

He stared at her, his attention snagged. "How do you figure?"

"The same people who lost the *Hasty Breeze* were the ones murdered. What are the chances? I don't believe in coincidences."

Now that she'd mentioned it, neither did he. At the time, he'd been so angry with the whole getting arrested thing that he hadn't calmed down enough to think about the case logically. But what she suggested made a lot of sense.

"Okay, say you're right. What then?"

"Then," she said, picking up her drink with a flourish, "in order to get the cops hot on the trail of the real murderer instead of you, all we have to do is to tell them to find your missing yacht!"

Seemed like a win-win to him. "Okay, why not. Let's go back and tell them."

As it turned out, it was not that easy. Not that Sean had really expected it to be. Things never were.

After finishing their meal, he and Zoë took a taxi back to the police station and asked to speak with Sanjit again. But the detective inspector barely listened to Sean's suggestion of a connection between the murders and the missing boat, and dismissed them with a rude slash of the hand. "I don't have the manpower for a wild-goose chase," he stated imperiously. "Especially when I already know who the killer is."

"Oh?" Zoë said, perking up. "Who?"

Sanjit pointed at Sean. "Him."

With a huff, she started to make a different kind of

suggestion, so Sean thanked the inspector politely and hauled her out of there pronto, before *she* got arrested.

But the whole incident did convince him of one thing. She was right. He might have to solve this case himself, or he really could end up in prison convicted of a double homicide. He loved Fiji but he wasn't naive. He knew how justice could work in third-world countries, and true guilt or innocence wasn't always the bottom line. Fiji depended heavily on tourism. An American convicted of killing other Americans would look good in the media and satisfy potential visitors that the murders had nothing to do with the country itself. Everyone was happy. Except Sean.

Damn. He *so* did not need this right now.

"Okay. I'll just have to find that damned boat myself," he grumbled, handing Zoë into the taxi that waited to take them back to the marina once again.

"You mean *we*."

Climbing in after her, he made a mental list of the instructions he'd have to give Aruna for the next few days. There wouldn't be many. Luckily the inn's hostess already knew more than he did about running a bed-and-breakfast.

"*We* what?" he asked distractedly.

"The boat. I'm coming with you."

"Right." She still had to get home. "Sure, I'll drop you off at the Indigo before heading out on my search."

"No. I mean I'm coming *with* you. To look for your missing yacht."

Whoa. He shook his head. "Not a chance."

"Why not? I can't finish the Indigo's evaluation anyway until your full staff reports. Spending a few days island-hopping will be fun. An adventure."

He frowned. Aside from the whole getting-a-bit-too-close-to-a-relationship-for-comfort thing, they were talking about tracking down a murderer.

"Are you forgetting this guy has killed two people? If we're right and there is a connection, finding that yacht could be a very dangerous proposition. I don't want you involved."

"Oh, but it's fine for you to risk getting hurt?"

"It's my yacht."

Her face took on a mulish cast. "You need backup."

"Not you."

"Why not?"

"I told you—"

"As soon as we find it we'll call the police," she interrupted. "Everyone stays safe. Sean, you are *not* going out there by yourself."

He pressed his lips together. She was playing dirty by calling him Sean and not Breeze. Breeze could blow off her concerns. Not Sean.

"Besides, I thought you wanted me to exercise my good judgment. How can I do that if you leave me behind?" Her lips curved in a meaningful smile.

Oh, now she was *really* playing dirty.

Too bad his body didn't care that it was being manipulated. It reacted hard and fast to that very feminine smile. Unfortunately, the taxi arrived at the marina before he could do anything about it.

He glared at her as he paid the driver, but she just smiled wider. She knew she had him.

"You're on," he growled low in her ear as he guided her to the slips where he kept his rental yachts moored. "You want adventure? I'll give you a damn adventure."

He'd just have to keep her safe. The truth was, having her along would probably ensure he didn't end up with his throat slit on a beach somewhere due to his temper. Not a bad trade-off.

She'd keep him in check and he'd keep her safe.

Meanwhile they'd keep each other naked. And both would exercise their very best judgment.

They'd find the *Hasty Breeze* and the real killer, clear his name, then at the end of the week he'd put her on a plane to her next assignment, and his life would get back to normal.

Naked, safe, then gone, he promised himself.

Yep. That would work.

Having grown up on a dairy farm, Zoë didn't know a thing about yachts. But the *Summer Breeze*—she was beginning to see a pattern here—was sleek and beautiful and she could see how proud Sean was of her. Her, because according to him all boats were female. Watching him caress the smooth, molded fiberglass curves and gleaming wood trim of the yacht with his strong hands as he showed her around the deck almost made Zoë jealous.

Ridiculous.

Zoë never got jealous. And certainly not of a stupid boat.

Which was why it shocked her as much as it did him when they went below and he opened the door to the master cabin and she pushed him inside and toppled him onto his back on the bed and crawled on top of him before either of them knew what was happening.

She looked down into his surprised but expectant face…and totally lost her nerve.

"Don't stop now," he urged just as she was about to bail. "I can't wait to see what comes next."

That made two of them. She felt her cheeks blaze. Honestly, she wasn't like this. But damn it, she'd started this affair and was determined to enjoy it while it lasted. So she manned-up, leaned down and kissed him.

Immediately all her awkward shyness vanished in the melting warmth of his mouth. Lord, she loved how he kissed.

And she loved the leashed power of his masculine body as he held her tight and returned her kiss with long, slow strokes of his tongue. She loved the way he smelled, and the low groans he made deep in his throat when she started to touch him. And especially the quivers she felt up and down her body when he touched her back.

Sweet mercy, if she didn't watch out she could easily fall for the man. Fall hard.

But what woman could guard her heart when he was kissing her so exquisitely as he peeled off her clothes, and she was loving the feel of his hard body against hers as he thrust deep into her?

Time enough to guard her heart when their few days together were up. Until then she would throw herself into the thrill of being with him, and hope like hell her heart would come out the other side in one piece.

She was shameless.

Sean had made love to her until she was a limp puddle of satiety and then kissed her one last time, gone up on deck and gotten the *Summer Breeze* underway. Zoë didn't know how he could even move, let alone maneuver a twenty-foot yacht out of the marina, power away from Vanua Levu and cruise out into the open sea. She watched the scenery pass by the high portholes in the master cabin lying exhausted on the bed with a loopy smile on her face, trying to work up the energy to join him on deck. When she finally got it together to get dressed she realized the only clothes she had with her were the dress and panties scattered on the floor.

So she swiped up the bottle of sunblock sitting on the nightstand and climbed the ladder to the deck without a stitch on.

When Sean turned from the wheel to greet her he actually dropped his beer. Then he grinned and opened his arms to her. "Woman, you are truly a fantasy come true. Come here."

He wasn't so bad himself in nothing but a pair of short blue swimming trunks and dark aviator sunglasses that glinted in the bright sunshine, his unruly hair streaming behind, steady on his feet despite the fast motion of the boat churning through the waves. The diving knife sheathed at his hip added just the right touch of danger.

She went into his arms and shivered with delight at the feel of him. So tall and broad and strong. He kissed her deeply and caressed her curves, and even though they'd just made love it was obvious they both wanted to do it again.

Pulling back, he gave her a drowning look and a lover's smile and a deep male growl rumbled in his chest. "Baby, what you do to me should be illegal."

"I believe it is in several states," she murmured

softly, drawing his earlobe into her mouth as she slid his trunks down over his thighs.

He groaned. "Damn good thing we're in Fiji." His expression turned predatory. "Turn around."

With one swift, powerful hand he bent her over the captain's chair and with the other gave her a sharp slap on the bottom. She gasped at the sting. But before the sound had even reached her throat he thrust into her from behind and the pain turned to acute pleasure.

The speeding boat plunged through a wave, peppering them with salty spray. The wind whipped them and the sun beat down on her back as he wound his hand in her hair and took her hard and fast.

She couldn't think, could only hang on to the captain's chair and let herself go, give herself over to the sensual, thrilling experience of being with this man. And try to ignore the voice inside telling her that *this* was the adventure, *he* was the excitement she'd been seeking all her life, not some meaningless job. And bury the fact that all too soon her time with him would be over.

"Stay with me, sweetheart," he commanded as he pumped into her over and over, bringing them both higher and higher, closer and closer to blissful release. And suddenly she realized she didn't want it to end. Ever.

The boat sped and the wind whipped and he scythed, and she knew that *this* was what she wanted from her life. *He* was what she wanted.

"No!" she cried. Impossible.

"Yes," he growled, and another smack landed on her bottom, exploding into a kaleidoscope of pleasure-pain. "Come with me now, baby. Give yourself over."

She came with a blinding sob, splintered in a million pieces. And knew with shattering insight that this affair was not going to end well. At least, not for her.

Chapter 9

Strange.

For Zoë the sex had been so explosive on every level that her protective instincts must have kicked in because right after Sean's damn-that-was-good kiss, she excused herself to clean up and practically ran down the ladder to the cabin to get away from him.

Oh, God. Oh, God. *Oh, God.*

What had just happened to her? Was she *crazy* thinking those thoughts about wanting him? The man's name was *Breeze,* for crying out loud! And he'd made it pretty damn clear he was in it for the short haul with no interest in extending her stay. Hello? Of *course* it would end badly. At least if she invested any emotional attachment to him.

The key was not to invest.

Was it too late?

No. It wasn't. Sure, he was amazing, and yes, she was having an incredible time with him. The South Seas setting was killer. The sex was to die for. The man was a walking, talking temptation. What woman wouldn't lose her way around him? But she was not in love with Sean Guthrie. She *wasn't*. And she would never give up her job and her life back home to be with him. Even if he wanted her to. Which he didn't. And never would.

So that was settled. And she was totally cool with it.

Really.

Truly.

But the strange part was when she finally settled herself down, told herself she was being silly and took herself back up on deck—still nude, to prove to herself she was over her foolishness once and for all—it almost seemed as if Sean was trying to distance himself, too.

Oh, he kissed her warmly enough when she appeared at his side, teased her appreciatively about her daring and refused to let her get dressed even though he'd slipped his trunks back on, then slanted her wait-'til-I-get-you-back-in-bed looks whenever their eyes met.

But he was avoiding her. She could feel it.

As the boat plowed through the open sea on auto pilot, he cleaned up his spilled beer and messed with the ropes and controls, checked charts and radioed in to the marina to let them know he'd taken the *Summer Breeze* and inform them where he'd be, and to expect George and Jeela's brothers to turn up and take one of the unreserved boats, which apparently any of the villagers were welcome to do at anytime. All the while he didn't touch her more than once or twice as she spread a towel on deck, lathered on a ton of sunblock and lay down to bask in the warm sun. He'd even frowned for a nanosecond when she'd asked him to do her back.

Definitely distancing himself.

She sighed inwardly. Time for some reassurances.

"Where are we headed?" she asked when he handed her an icy beer and settled back in the captain's chair under the canopy, kicking his feet up on the cooler and pulling the brim of a *Summer Breeze* souvenir baseball cap low over his dark glasses. Nothing like being obvious or anything.

"Taveuni. Though I thought I'd check out a few of the smaller islands on the way," he said gruffly.

I, not *we*, she noted. "Why Taveuni?"

"Third-largest island in Fiji. Lots of shallow reefs to smash up on and plenty of isolated stretches of jungle along the coast if you're looking to hide."

"Which are you voting for?"

He shook his head. "If I knew that, I'd know where to start looking. If I don't pick up any leads I'll probably head around to Qamea."

Again with the *I*.

"The scene of the crime," she murmured.

"I want to nose around the resort. Check out the other patrons, in case the Blantons talked to someone about what really happened to the *Hasty Breeze*."

"And if that doesn't pan out?"

"I've charted out a search grid, hitting all the islands within a fifty-mile radius. Boats that big don't just disappear. Somewhere, someone's got to have seen it."

She took a deep breath. "Just remember I need to be back to the Indigo in time to finish my evaluation before leaving this weekend." Though her heart squeezed, she said it casually. Like the only thing she was worried about was getting out of there on time.

He glanced up and regarded her neutrally. Was that fleeting glint in his eyes one of relief? That she had no designs on his feelings or his future? That she was still all about the sex and not remotely thinking of a picket fence?

A prick of pain lanced through her. Damn. Well, she'd warned herself what could happen if she slept with him.

Not a problem. She could take it. She just had to focus on the dream job she'd cared so much about only yesterday. That was enough. That was plenty. All she'd ever wanted.

Until today.

But today wouldn't last, and if she hadn't known it before, the indifferent look on Breeze's face said it all.

"I remember," he said, then tipped his beer up and took a long pull, his gaze drifting off to the turquoise waves.

Okay, then.

She closed her eyes and pretended to sleep. All the while fighting not to cry.

Stupid. Stupid, stupid, stupid.

The tension between them didn't go away as the afternoon dragged on. If anything, it got worse.

The yacht sped along at a fast clip, eating up the miles on the circuitous route to Taveuni, slowing only at the small, unpopulated islands along the way. Those, they circled around with binoculars, carefully searching for a telltale flash of white-and-blue fiberglass on the shallow reefs or hidden in a dozen tiny jungle-draped lagoons. They found nothing. For each island they crossed off his list, the crankier Sean got.

"We'll find it," Zoë assured him, reapplying sunblock for the third time. "I promise. You just have to be patient."

He just scowled at her and popped another beer.

Whatever. She yawned and closed her eyes, emotionally drained from the sleepless night, the crazy morning and the tension-filled afternoon. Inwardly, she was still fighting to keep it together, but she refused to be cranky.

Hell, she'd had the best night of sex in her entire life with the most incredible…if moody…man she'd ever met; the sun was warm on her naked body and the sea spray in her face was refreshing. How many women were lucky enough to experience so much perfection at one time? She simply refused to be depressed.

She stole another glance at Sean, who was sprawled in his captain's chair with his corded arms crossed over his drool-worthy chest staring out to sea. It was all she could do to keep herself from giving in and jumping him again.

Down, girl. She'd probably scare him even further away if she made another move like that. Let him come to her next time. Except she'd probably be waiting until doomsday for that to happen, given his present mood.

Ah, well. A girl could dream, couldn't she?

So, with a determinedly content smile on her face, she closed her eyes again and proceeded to do just that.

* * *

She'd fallen asleep.

Naked.

The damn woman had fallen asleep on him. *Naked.* Lying there all exposed on her bright green towel with one arm flung over her head, her golden hair disheveled from the breeze—yeah, both kinds, he taunted himself—and her tawny lashes fanned over her bronzy-pink cheeks. Had he mentioned she was completely naked?

And driving him out of his mind with lust.

Along with something else. Something far more disturbing. Something he didn't want to think about. Something that terrified him so much he'd avoided her luscious naked body all afternoon, hoping the terror would go away.

It hadn't.

God *damn* it.

He was falling for her.

He, Sean never-again-in-this-lifetime-will-I-*ever*-fall-in-love Guthrie, was falling for a woman who only wanted to use him for a few days of hot sex, and then fly blithely off into the sunset without looking back.

How the hell had *that* happened?

Well, naturally he knew how it had happened. He'd told her he wasn't interested and she'd told him she *certainly* wasn't interested, but they'd both lied. So he'd seduced her anyway. And got caught in his own damn net.

His bad.

Why, oh, why had he let her come along on this excursion? The damn woman was relentlessly sexy, incurably soft and pliant, and so damn arousing he'd been walking around like a freaking whale harpoon all day.

Slamming down his untouched beer, he jumped up and stalked over to where she was stretched out on the deck asleep. Her lush body was the color of golden honey, except for the paler areas where she normally wore a bikini. Her bare skin glistened with a tantalizing mix of suntan oil, sweat and sea spray. Her pretty white breasts rose and fell evenly; her legs reposed slightly apart, revealing a tantalizing glimpse of her hidden sex.

A rush of possessiveness washed over him. He had been there. He had owned that sweet body, for a short while. It gave him a primitive satisfaction that other men were denied this vision of her—naked, relaxed, willing.

He stood at her feet and ached to take her again. To spread her thighs wide and ram himself into her to the very hilt. To do it over and over until she screamed with pleasure, begging him to do it again and again and again until neither of them could move and she would never, ever think of leaving him again.

He clenched his jaw.

In her sleep she swallowed and sighed, murmuring a soft sound that nearly brought him to his knees. "*Sean...*"

Had she really whispered his name?

Bald emotion razored through his heart. *Damn!* How could he even be thinking what he was thinking? How could he consider trusting another woman with his feelings after what had happened last time? His heart couldn't take the pain. Not again. And Zoë had made it clear where her priorities lay. Love was not on her to-do list.

Which was both a blessing and a curse.

Her eyes fluttered open and her gaze met his. He didn't smile, didn't move. Just watched her. Her lips parted a fraction. After an endless, silent moment, she slowly opened her legs. Inviting him in.

He swallowed heavily. He shouldn't. But he couldn't stop himself. Unstrapping his knife and easing his trunks down over his insatiable, out-of-control arousal, he let them both fall to the deck. The pulse in her neck was beating wildly as he went to his knees, then dropped to all fours above her.

You're mine, he thought ferociously, but didn't dare say the words aloud. For fear he couldn't take them back. For fear she would laugh. For fear they would never be true.

Her hands shook when she put them tentatively on his chest, as though she were suddenly terrified to touch him. Probably smart. He was feeling like a wild beast. He could feel every ripple of his roped muscles as he grasped her thighs and parted them wider, feel every strain of tense movement as he positioned his tall frame over her trembling, smaller body, feel every dark breath in his lungs as he covered and mounted her in a deep, claiming burst of power.

A cry stuttered from her lips and her arms went around his neck. Her legs wrapped about his waist.

She was his.

His.

"Mine," he growled.

"Yes," she whispered.

And that's when he lost control.

Afterward, Sean rolled Zoë on top of him so she wouldn't be crushed beneath his weight. His heart was pumping like a locomotive. He desperately needed to get away from this. From her. But he didn't want to let her go. He held her tight against his chest and pressed his lips firmly to her temple.

Neither of them spoke. It was as though both of them were taken aback, shocked into an edgy silence by the overwhelming intensity of their lovemaking. It had been basic. Primal. Almost savage. There had been nothing tender in his taking of her. He'd wanted and he'd taken. She had opened herself and given. He'd gorged himself on her like a starving animal, and she had eagerly fed his hunger with her bounty.

His body throbbed with repletion and yet he wanted more.

He wanted to run like hell, and yet he wanted to cling to her like a miser clings to gold.

In the end it was civilization that roused them from their paralysis. The distant sound of music and laughter floated across the water, snagging his attention and lifting his head. He scanned the horizon with narrowed eyes.

They were approaching Taveuni.

Chapter 10

Zoë almost welcomed the intrusion into the chaos that arced between her and Sean, forcing them to take a giant step back from the sense of impending panic that vibrated the very air around them after they'd made love—or whatever it was they'd just done.

Almost. Because her female urge to communicate, to hash things out, felt acutely frustrated. But…shutting that door was probably just as well. Talking and hashing would do neither of them any good. It was what it was. And what it was, was explosive…and temporary.

So she went below, quickly showered in the microscopic cabinette, pulled her dress over her head and stroked on some lipstick and mascara. There. Back to normal. Well, as normal as she could be without underwear.

Except her body didn't feel normal. She could still sense the imprint of Sean's powerful hands on it, holding and caressing, his tongue licking and his teeth biting. Even after her shower, the scent of him clung to her skin, claiming her, marking her as his. His possession. *His mate*.

Except of course she wasn't. And she needed to get over it.

She turned from the mirror and caught him watching her from beneath a dark scowl. He must have jumped into the ocean to wash because his tawny hair was wet and sticking out from being rubbed with a towel. His skin was beaded with drops of water. He'd put on a pair of low-riding jeans and clutched a deep blue shirt in his fist.

"You're going to wrinkle that," she said, the first words she'd uttered for hours. Other than crying out his name earlier. Her face heated at the swift, dazzling memory.

His gaze jerked from her cheeks down to the wrinkled shirt in his hand. He shrugged and slipped it over his wet shoulders, then raked his fingers through his long hair. "Ready?"

She glanced out of the porthole and saw a clutch of low thatched roofs. He must have tied up at a dock while she was in the shower. "As ever," she replied.

It turned out they'd put in at a fancy gated community attached to an exclusive resort and golf club that catered to the wealthy expatriates who lived on the picture-perfect garden island. At the clubhouse Sean was greeted like an old friend, one obviously well-acquainted with the predominantly male patrons gathered at the bar for their nineteenth hole—who proceeded to slap him on the back and joke about his being arrested for murder. News apparently traveled fast in the Fiji expat community. But the men clearly did not take the charge seriously. Curious eyes turned to Zoë as he introduced her to them as his "friend," but brows raised knowingly when he kept a proprietary arm firmly around her waist.

She could just imagine the conversation that ensued after an elegant Frenchwoman named Madame Cuvet strolled in and Sean smoothly finessed her into taking Zoë "shopping" at a trio of swanky clothing boutiques that flanked the lobby of the club.

"I completely ruined two of Zoë's dresses," he explained to a rumble of masculine chuckles. A singularly unapologetic curl graced his lips as he kissed her on the cheek and told Madame Cuvet, "Help her pick out something pretty."

Zoë really wanted to kick him in the shins. But instead she smiled sweetly and played along, in the faint hope that his true purpose was to get her to quiz the Frenchwoman about the Blantons—the whole reason they were there.

But Madame dismissed the subject of missing boats with an impatient flick of her manicured fingers, ignored Zoë's repeated protests that she had no intention of allowing "*Monsieur* Breeze" to buy her anything whatsoever, and marched her into the nearest boutique. There the woman proceeded to ply her with French champagne and hold one amazing dress after another up to her until declaring, "*Voilà, ce'st ça,*" or words to that effect.

Zoë wasn't exactly sure, since her high school French was rusty at best, but she figured she'd made her point when after the third boutique and their fourth flute of champagne, the woman rattled off a torrent of French to the poor Fijian saleslady then herded Zoë back to the club bar with not a single glittery bag in tow. But in a much better mood.

Zoë felt so much more relaxed she didn't even mind when Sean greeted her by rising—well, all the men did, such gentlemen—and guided her into his vacated leather fauteuil, placing a fairly blatant kiss on her neck while taking a seat on the fat arm of her chair, where he perched until ten or fifteen minutes later, then turned to her with a smile and asked if she'd like to freshen up before having dinner with his friends and their wives.

She smiled back and nodded, figuring it was just an excuse to make their escape. Imagine her surprise when a valet in a golf cart drove them to a lavish *bure*—one of those romantic open-sided thatched huts that was built on a wooden walkway over the clear blue water of the bay— and Sean announced they were spending the night there.

"But what about our search?" she asked, pushing aside a pile of gold beribboned boxes to plop down on the huge, satin-draped bed that filled the back portion of the *bure*. The room was exquisitely beautiful and so dreamily romantic it stole her breath away.

"It'll be dark soon anyway," he said, gesturing to the Technicolor sunset framed in the open seaward side of the *bure* like a picture postcard. The shimmering swath of red-orange painted above the blue, blue sea was captivatingly lovely.

"My God, you're lucky to live in this place," she said, sighing with the envy of a traveler who'd found a piece of paradise she knew she'd have to leave all too soon.

"You could stay," he said without inflection, poking through the boxes behind her on the bed. "You could live here, too."

She turned to look at him, but he wasn't paying any attention to her. Stifling another sigh, she turned back to the sunset. "Chicago's not so bad."

He grunted and pulled something out of one of the boxes. "This one, I think."

"Hmm?"

"Wear this one tonight. It'll go with my tie."

"What?" A slippery length of blue silk charmeuse poured into her lap. She recognized one of the gorgeous dresses she'd refused in the boutiques. She frowned at it. "Where did—" The glitter of gold and brilliant blue gemstones landed on top of the silk. She blinked, and gasped softly. A necklace. A very expensive necklace, by the look of it. "What on earth—"

"These people dress for dinner." He straightened, holding up an elegant tuxedo on a padded hanger. "Old school. Not my style, but what can you do."

Her jaw dropped. The black tux looked fresh off a Paris runway, and the dress in her lap, she recalled, carried a four-figure price tag. She didn't even want to think about what the necklace was worth. "Sean, this is absurd. Let's just have dinner on the *Summer Breeze*. I'm sure I can rustle up a can of chili or something."

He regarded her wryly. "You prefer canned chili to fresh lobster and sapphires?"

She pressed her lips together. Anyone would be insane to prefer that. But it wasn't the point. "These clothes have to cost nearly as much as your missing yacht. These people aren't worth it. What are you trying to prove to them?"

He stared at her, then gave a bark of laughter. "Nothing. I have nothing to prove to anyone. Now put on the damn dress and let's go eat."

She sat there waffling for so long he'd already stripped out of his jeans and zipped up the tux pants before taking her by the shoulders and compelling her to her feet.

"Do you want me to undress you?" he asked, giving her a look that made it clear he'd do it, but without the good stuff that usually followed.

"I don't understand you," she said.

The corner of his lip jerked. "Yeah, that makes two of us." He raised his hand and drew the tips of his fingers down the side of her face, tucking a strand of hair behind her ear. "Indulge me, Zoë. Just for tonight, pretend you're my woman and let me spoil you."

She squeezed her eyes shut, lest he see the yearning in them. "This is crazy. You know I'll be with you regardless."

"I know," he said. "But I want to do this."

She opened her eyes and mustered a small nod and a smile. "All right. For you."

She was stunning in blue. Madame Cuvet had picked well. Sean was pretty sure Zoë would look stunning no matter what she wore—or didn't wear—but the blue dress was spectacular on her. As were the sapphires and the small diamond earrings he'd found tucked into the toe of the sexy high heels that matched the long, curve-hugging dress. She was by far the most beautiful woman in all of Fiji tonight.

And every inch of her was his.

Tonight.

When he walked into the club with her on his arm, every eye in the place was on her. But the best thing was, her eyes were only for him. All through dinner she conversed with the circle of sophisticated, international men who competed for her attention, but her gaze would always seek his, her eyes soft and adoring. And afterward when the music started and he led her outside to the polished teak patio under the stars in the jasmine-scented night, she politely danced with the hopeful men who asked her, but only after glancing at him for his nod of approval, and all through the number she'd slant him coy looks until he couldn't stand it any longer and cut in, then she'd lower her lashes and nestle into his arms with a sigh, so much like a woman in love he almost forgot it was just pretend.

It felt so good just to be with her that he didn't even mind that not a single person in the place had ever heard of the Blantons, nor had anyone seen the *Hasty Breeze* on any of their recent deep-sea fishing trips or leisurely sailing excursions.

It just meant he and Zoë would have to continue their search tomorrow, as planned.

One more day to be with her.

One more day to torture himself.

One more day to wonder if he was doing the right thing by letting her leave when all was said and done.

"Shall I send for a golf cart?" he asked when he caught her yawning.

"Let's walk back," she said, taking his arm. "It's not that far."

"Sure?"

"Such a beautiful night. I don't want it to end."

He knew the feeling. It had been the strangest day of his life. Who knew that a day which started out with his being arrested for murder could end so well? Despite the torment of feelings roiling within him, he was so not ready for this day to be over yet.

When they got to the beach, Zoë kicked off her shoes and jumped from the wooden walkway onto the sand. "Last one in's a rotten egg," she called, hiking up her dress with a laugh and running through the silvery, ankle-deep tips of the waves.

He stuck his hands in his pants pockets and grinned. "You're nuts if you think I'm getting my new tux wet," he called back. "But you go right ahead."

"Spoilsport! Roll up the cuffs!" she yelled.

He grinned wider as she twirled in the shallow water. *Oh, what the hell*. He toed off his shoes, glad he'd dispensed with the unnecessary formality of socks, rolled up his pant legs to his calves and joined her.

"Here, hold this," she said, whirling up to him, and suddenly he was holding her blue dress in his hands. "I don't want to ruin it."

He froze in shock. Except for the sapphires and earrings she was completely nude. Because he'd selfishly wanted her to wear only his gifts tonight, nothing else. Damn, was he glad.

Something rustled in the thick vegetation that canted

the beach and he thought of the parrots. Muttering a low curse, he scanned the area. But nothing appeared, and the rustling abruptly stopped. To his relief not another soul was around, feathered or human. Good. This was one fantasy he had no intention of sharing.

She danced away from him, and he slung the dress over his shoulder, wishing it were her. "Come back here, you," he ordered, half-scandalized but fully aroused.

She stuck out her tongue at him and ran into the waves.

He clamped his teeth stubbornly. *Not* ruining the tux. Or the dress, now it was in his care. Bracing his feet apart, he put his hands on his hips and waited for her to come to him. She would. Eventually.

Meanwhile, she looked like a seductive sea nymph, playing in the waves wearing nothing but sapphires and a smile. Taunting him. Tempting him. Making him want things he had no business wanting.

She *would* come to him.

And he would make her want to stay.

He would make *her* want things she had no business wanting. Except he would give them all to her. And he'd open his heart and learn to trust again.

Eventually.

"Come here," he called.

She grinned and shook her head. "Come and get me."

He grinned back. "You'll come," he told her.

"I won't."

You will, he thought, and she cocked her head. "I'll make you come," he yelled.

And she grinned wider. "Promise?"

"Oh, yeah," he assured. "You can take that to the bank."

"But the water's so nice."

"I prefer dry land."

"But you own boats."

"And look how well that turned out."

In the moonlight she smiled sweetly. "We'll find it," she said.

"You keep saying that and here we are, no closer."

"You don't know that. It might be right around the corner."

"Boats don't do corners."

"You know what I mean."

"Yeah," he said. He was beginning to. And he had the sinking feeling it had nothing to do with boats.

Just when he felt the first edge of anger creep through his gut—or was it despair?—she came to him. And the sharpness melted into the warmth of her wet body as he pulled her close and banded his arms around her.

"Your tux," she protested, but not really, because she let him kiss her and wrap her in his jacket to dry the sea from her skin, and he couldn't care less about the stupid tux.

"What am I going to do with you?" he murmured.

She looked up at him and smiled, raised on her toes and whispered softly in his ear, making him smile, too.

"I can do that," he said.

And swept her up in his arms and carried her back to the *bure* and the big, satin-draped bed.

Chapter 11

"You two honeymooners better be careful out there. I hear another pair of lovebirds got sliced and diced by some maniac while they were making out on the beach a few weeks ago. Hell of a way to go."

Sean winced. They were at breakfast and the boisterous newcomer who'd made the remark was sitting at the next table. A good ol' boy named Tony, a buddy of one of the regular club members, on vacation fresh from the States. Obviously he hadn't gotten the memo about Sean's arrest.

Zoë's cheeks turned red, no doubt about the honeymooner thing. Sean chuckled politely along with the others and patted her hand reassuringly. "Thanks. We'll keep that in mind," he said to Tony, trying to avoid the whole can of worms. Several cans, actually.

But the man wouldn't shut up. "Yeah, I have a friend who's got a place over on American Samoa. Says the local cops are trying like crazy to hush it up, but everyone's all riled up about the killings. Guess the guy really did a number on that couple."

Sean stared at him in sudden confusion. Wait. The timing was all wrong, and so was the country. "American Samoa?"

"Yeah. Guess I'm not surprised y'all haven't heard about it over here on Fiji. Like I said, the local law—"

"Hey, Tony! Tee time!" somebody called from the pro shop door, and with a wave Tony jumped up and trotted off to his golf game.

Sean met Zoë's equally surprised look over her coffee cup. What the hell? There was *another* murdered couple? He rose abruptly. "We better get going, too. Long trip ahead of us."

He didn't have to ask her twice. Excitement hurried them both out of the dining room after hasty goodbyes.

"My God," she said. "Do you realize what this means?"

He tried to think logically. "It could just be a coincidence."

"Two couples? Both killed on the beach, within weeks of each other?"

"Thousands of miles apart," he reminded her. "The South Seas is a big place."

"I'm telling you, it's a serial killer!"

"Or maybe you've just been watching too many episodes of *Criminal Minds*."

"We need to tell the police," she said.

"Because it was so easy to convince them of our

theory last time. No, we need to find out more first."
But with any luck she was right, and Sanjit would
actually listen, and there would be one less potential
disaster hanging over Sean's head to worry about.

"Let's get back to the *Summer Breeze*," he said. "I'll
call Regi ship-to-shore so he can make some inquiries
and you use the laptop to see what you can find out on
the Internet. There should be Wi-Fi from the marina."

They went straight to the *bure* to gather their things.
Zoë suddenly stopped in front of the bed where they'd
spent the night in each other's arms, and turned to him.
Her face was filled with an emotion he couldn't begin
to decipher.

"What?" he asked.

"Last night was magical," she said, her voice husky.
"I'll never forget it as long as I live. Thank you, Sean."

The swift change in subject caught him unprepared.
"I— Me, neither," he said lamely, wanting nothing
more than to tug her into his embrace and hold her until
he had the courage to open himself up the way she had.
To say the things that crowded his mind.

But the moment was over as quickly as it began, and
she turned away to pick up the dresses and things he'd
bought for her yesterday and fold them into their gilt
boxes. He grimaced inwardly at his cowardice and
swiped up his tuxedo bag, following her onto the
wooden walkway as she strode out of the *bure*. She was
wearing another of Madame Cuvet's selections this
morning. A frothy, filmy dress with colorful flowers on
it. It was pretty, but he would have chosen something
shorter. Next time he'd take her shopping himself.

He prayed there'd be a next time.

They got to the *Summer Breeze* and each set about their appointed task. His call to Regi went smoothly. As soon as Sean told him what Tony had said, the lawyer grasped the situation immediately.

"I'll find out what I can, and let you know," Regi promised. "If we establish there's a serial killer at work, the authorities can't possibly suspect you any more."

Things were looking up.

Sean hung up the satellite phone and climbed down the ladder to the yacht's salon where Zoë was sitting on the couch peering at his laptop screen.

"Find anything?"

"Very little. There are a couple of mentions of the killings in an expat blog from about six weeks ago, but unfortunately just rumors, no real details."

"What about newspapers?"

"The two online ones from American Samoa are pretty thin on news. Nothing about the murders at all."

He nodded and perched on the sofa arm. "Not unexpected, I suppose. Regi should be able to ferret out something from his contacts."

She sighed and closed the laptop. "I can't believe the authorities are being so closemouthed about this. And obviously not sharing information. People should be warned."

"Different countries. A jurisdictional nightmare. And tourism's a big deal in this neck of the woods. Grisly murders tend to keep travelers away."

She looked up. "So what do we do now?"

Looking into her pretty face, he knew what he'd like to do. They'd already done it about a hundred times in the past forty-eight hours, but he was ready again.

He hardly recognized himself. He'd turned into a genuine sex maniac around her. Not that she seemed to be complaining. He certainly wasn't.

However, in light of this new information, it was more important than ever to find his missing yacht. If this psycho had taken it… Well, the thought of a serial killer using the *Hasty Breeze* for some sick purpose, or even only as transportation to a new venue, made Sean physically ill.

"Let's continue our search as planned," he said grimly. "We'll just have to be extra careful if we find anything."

They didn't find the *Hasty* that morning as they cruised north up the Taveuni coast, scanning the reefs and many small bays, and stopping briefly at the few tiny villages along the way. Nor did they find it that afternoon. In the evening they docked at another posh resort at the other end of the island, and oddly enough, ran into Tony again.

"Hey, buddy, small world," the tall man boomed from a stool at the bar, beckoning them over. "Any luck finding that boat of yours?"

"Not yet," Sean responded, battening down a sudden spurt of suspicion. Odd, the guy showing up here. The world wasn't *that* small. Or maybe it was, and Sean was just being paranoid. "Thought you were playing golf today?"

"Got a better offer. Doin' some deep-sea fishing with my new friends." He waved at a youngish couple Sean recognized from last night relaxing with a few others outside on the deck. "You two lovebirds like to

join us for dinner? Or would you rather be alone…?"
He winked at Zoë, who promptly turned red again.

Sean already had his arm around her, but at that las-
civious wink his protective instincts burst forth and he
pulled her tight against his side.

"We'd love to join you," Zoë answered, to his
chagrin.

But, despite Sean's misgivings, that turned out to be
a very good thing because when he casually brought up
the subject of the missing yacht during dessert, one of
the older men in the group thought he remembered
seeing a boat answering the description of the *Hasty
Breeze* tucked deep in a hidden cove down the coast in
the Bouma National Park—on the side of the island
they hadn't searched yet.

"When was this?" Sean asked the man.

He thought about it for a minute. "Had to have been
day before yesterday."

So the day after the murders. That fit. The *Hasty
Breeze* was a fast little vessel, and the killer would have
wanted to get away from the scene of the crime as
quickly as possible. *If* the *Hasty* wasn't smashed up on
some totally unrelated reef, Sean reminded himself,
and fervently hoped that was the case despite mounting
evidence to the contrary.

After a nightcap they made their way back to the
Summer Breeze. "We'll leave first thing in the morning," he told Zoë, helping her make the short jump
from the dock to the deck.

He'd wanted to get them a nice room at the resort,
but she said she didn't feel like packing an overnight

bag, and besides, she insisted, they had a perfectly good bed onboard, so why not use it?

He still hadn't gotten used to how different Zoë was from his ex-wife, who would have insisted he obtain the best suite in the resort and woe betide the poor slobs who might already occupy the room. Her nickname wasn't Her Royal Roxanne for nothing.

But Zoë was nothing like that, he was slowly learning. Which only made him want to lavish her with even more gifts and luxuries. With his ex-wife he'd felt forced and obligated. With Zoë, giving her things was a joy and a pleasure.

Because she'd already given him so much. Sex, yes. Killer sex. But a lot more than that. More important things, like help, support and companionship. Her unflappable joie de vivre had shaken him up, awakened his soul again to all he'd been missing out on. He hadn't realized how incredibly lonely he'd been these past years in Fiji. Sure, he'd had women come through his world. But none for more than a few days, nor had they really meant anything to him. His whole attention had been concentrated on the never-ending hard work required to rebuild his lost fortune and restore stability to his life. He'd been so narrowly focused he'd lost sight of the reason behind wanting those things— simple happiness.

Was it because the last piece of that restoration was almost in place that he'd finally started the painful process of opening himself to the possibility of love again? Had Zoë attracted his attention because, professionally, she was the key to that vital last step? Or was she really as perfect as she seemed?

The scary question was, was he truly ready for this? Or was he just setting himself up for massive disappointment once again…because *she* wasn't ready for this…? She might be acting like a woman in love, but he'd noticed she hadn't changed her outbound flight.

"You're being quiet," she said into the silence that had fallen over them. They were cuddled together on a lounger up on the top deck sipping wine and watching the stars. "What are you thinking about?"

"You," he said.

She glanced up at him with a little-girl smile. "Good things, I hope."

"I was remembering you on the beach last night. How you took off all your clothes. That was very naughty."

Her smile curved. "I thought you liked it when I'm naughty."

"Damn straight. I was hoping you'd do it again."

She slanted him a look. "You mean now?"

He so needed a distraction from his emotional roller coaster, from the questions dogging him, and couldn't think of a better diversion. He glanced around at the other boats moored along the dock. They were all dark and empty.

"Now."

She sat up and in a lithe movement drew her frothy dress up over her head and let it drop to the deck. She glanced over her shoulder at him. Oh, yeah. That's what he was talking about. He smiled and unfastened her bra, tossing it on top of the dress.

"Sit between my legs," he ordered, and while she was sliding over, her back to his front, he slipped off her panties and tossed them, too.

She wriggled back against him. His body quickened with a thrill of powerful arousal, and he ran his hands over her bare, silken flesh, cupping her generous breasts and slipping his fingers into her honeyed center.

"*Damn*, woman, what you do to me."

He loved how she obeyed him. Loved how she felt, naked and vulnerable in his arms. Loved how she eagerly submitted to his possession. And especially he loved how she loved him, fully and unabashedly.

How could he not fall completely in love with her in return?

Her body quivered and she hummed out a soft whimper as he touched her, letting her legs fall open. "More," she whispered.

He gladly obliged. Spreading her wide with one hand, teasing her with the other, circling and probing, rubbing and pinching, until she was drenched with excitement, writhing and panting, and begging him to finish her. But he took his time. Knowing her body well by now, he knew just how to make it last and last. Driving her crazy. Driving himself crazy, wanting to throw her under him and thrust into her, hard and thick, and slake the ravenous need within him to claim her totally, once and for all.

While he was thinking of himself, of what he would do to her when it was his turn, she came apart. She cried out and he forgot everything else to make it perfect for her, coaxing every last shuddering wave of pleasure and delight from her body.

"Good?" he asked when she finally opened her eyes and gave a long, low moan.

"So good. Oh, Sean, so incredibly good."

"I'm glad." He kissed her hair, and suddenly his own satisfaction wasn't nearly so important. In fact, nothing was as important as keeping this woman right where she was, all for himself. "Stay with me, baby," he murmured. "Move to Fiji and be with me."

Her body went perfectly still. She may even have stopped breathing. "But…we hardly know each other," she said softly.

"Plenty of time for that."

"My job—"

"Quit," he said, the command coming out before he considered what he was saying. The implications. It just felt right. "You don't need to work. I'll take care of you."

Slowly, she leaned forward and half turned to face him. "Sean, what are you asking here? Are you talking…"

She didn't say it, but the unspoken word swept through him like a sobering slap of ice water. *Marriage.* He blanched. *Whoa.* No, that wasn't what he'd meant. Definitely not ready for that step. Damn!

The next instant, the question in her expression dissolved and she turned away again, settling back against him. "We had an understanding when we started this affair. Neither of us wants to get involved. You're a mess and my career is too important to me. Remember?"

He could have sworn, for just a second when he'd first spoken, that she had wanted him to mean marriage. That her eyes had held shock, but also hopefulness. He must have been mistaken.

Thank God.

He wanted her like crazy. And he sure didn't want to hurt her. That was the last thing he wanted. But… marriage… The very idea terrified him.

And yet, the thought of her leaving him, it made him want to roar with anger and frustration.

"Zoë, we *are* involved," he insisted. "What's wrong with extending that for a few weeks, or months, or however long we feel like staying together?"

"Because," she said calmly, "afterwards you'll still be a mess, but I will no longer have a career."

She had him there. He blew out a long breath. "This sucks," he said.

"Yeah," she said. "It does."

It was too late. Far too late to distance herself emotionally.

She'd almost blown it. Luckily, the horrified look on Sean's face when Zoë very nearly brought up the idea of a commitment between them had been enough to freeze her tongue in its tracks.

Free as the breeze. She really had to remember that.

But Zoë was woman enough to admit, at least to herself, that she'd fallen totally, irrevocably in love with the man, and there was nothing at all she could do about it. Nothing she *wanted* to do about it, truth be told. It was the giddiest, dizziest, most wonderful feeling in the world. The fact that he didn't reciprocate was heart-breaking, crushingly so, but that didn't stop her own feelings. The end of their affair would come soon enough, and she would be devastated, but she wasn't ready to think about that yet. Until the time came to leave him, she was prepared to surrender completely to the amazing experience of loving the man of her dreams.

That night she made love to him. Genuine love. Pouring her whole heart into the physical act, she showed him with her body what her mouth didn't dare say.

But when at last he slept, spooned close against her back with his arms holding her tight and his deep rhythmic breaths stirring warm and sweet in her hair, she felt a single tear trickle down her cheek. And with a wistful sigh, she whispered the words she wished with all her heart he wanted to hear.

"I love you."

Chapter 12

"I don't freaking believe it."

Zoë looked up from the naval chart of Fiji she was studying and glanced at the stretch of jungled coast where Sean was training his binoculars. A small white-and-blue boat was moored in the sheltered lagoon. On the prow, painted in fancy script, she could just make out the word *Breeze*.

She jumped up. "Oh, my God! Is that it?"

Sean lowered the binoculars and jetted out a breath. "No. That's the *Welcome Breeze*. Damn!"

She blinked. "*Another* of your yachts? How many do you own, anyway?"

"Seven."

Okay, wow. "All named *Breeze*, I suppose."

He spared her a grin. "Too obsessive?"

She rolled her eyes. "Ya think?"

"Hmm. I didn't know the *Welcome* was rented this week. Before we left the marina I got a list of the boats that are out, and she wasn't on it." He swept the binoculars back to the lagoon. "Ah. It's the guys. Jeela's brothers and George. That explains it. They must be fishing. I'm glad he calmed down and took my advice."

Zoë grasped the rail and leaned on it, gazing in at the little boat, feeling a stab of sympathy. "Poor kid. He must be hurting." She could relate.

Not going there.

Sean shot her a look. "I thought you were on the girl's side."

"I was. I am." What a difference a few days made. "Hell, I'm on both their sides. Love is a real bitch."

"Tell me about it," he muttered. "Sex is so much easier."

All righty, then.

She took a cleansing breath. Not *going* there! "So. Does this mean the man at the club *didn't* see the *Hasty Breeze* hidden along here?"

Sean drilled a hand through his hair. "God knows."

"If the boys have been fishing around the island, maybe they spotted it," she suggested.

"It's possible."

"Maybe we should we go and ask them."

Zoë held her breath as Sean steered the *Summer Breeze* expertly through a narrow channel in the coral reef that scalloped the edges of the waters along the coast. Lord, she loved watching him concentrate. He was so good at everything he did. So focused.

So damn good-looking, too. Especially with his shirt off and the wind in his hair and the sun kissing his bronzed skin. Irresistibly sexy, that's what he was. The perfect embodiment of the hunky surfer-dude, but all grown up with a man's body. She wished to God she had a camera to capture this moment forever. So she could pull out the photo on the cold, snowy Chicago nights to come, and dream herself back to today.

Unfortunately, her memories would have to do.

"Hey, girl, you checkin' me out?"

"Put it on display you gotta expect it to get ogled."

He grinned at her, standing at the wheel against the wind like a sea captain of old. "See anything you like?"

She grinned back. "Plenty."

"You could take a closer look."

"You don't have that kind of time."

He gave a low, rumbling hum. "Sweet thing, I've got all the time in the world for you."

"Not if you want to avoid crashing two of your boats in one fell swoop," she said, jerking her thumb ahead.

He swore, and pulled back on the throttle, slowing and turning aside just in time to miss the *Welcome Breeze*. She hadn't been worried. How starstruck was that?

"*M'bula*, Mr. Breeze!" Jeela's little brother called from the other deck, waving with a broad smile as Sean brought the two boats to rest side-by-side, cushion fenders squeaking. "You come fishing with us, Miss?"

"*Bula*, guys," Sean called, waving back. "Any luck?"

"Nothing today," George said, folding his arms with a scowl. "But yesterday we almost caught a poacher. A woman poacher."

The older brother shifted on his feet. "It would have made no difference, man. Jeela is married now."

George gave a shrug. "My ancestors would have cooked and eaten him for what he did. But you are right, Mr. Breeze. There are many other women in the world."

Beneath her smile, Zoë ground her teeth. She *so* did not need a lesson in "Mr. Breeze's" philosophy of love right now.

Suddenly, Sean came to attention. "What's that?" He indicated a small cooler sitting in the shade of the bimini.

She looked closer. Just a cooler. It wasn't until the boys started shuffling their feet again that she realized with a start the name emblazoned on the lid was not *Welcome Breeze,* but *Hasty Breeze.* She let out a gasp. "Oh!"

"Hold her steady," Sean ordered her, relinquishing the wheel and leaping over the rail to the other boat. He halted just before grabbing the cooler. "Where did you find this?"

The older brother waved down the coast. "On the beach. Further south. About five miles."

"When?"

"Yesterday."

"Did you see any sign of the *Hasty Breeze?*"

They all shook their heads. "No," George said. "It was not there. Is something wrong? We knew the cooler belongs to you so we fetched it back."

Sean nodded somberly. "Thanks, guys. I appreciate that." He kneeled down on the balls of his feet and squinted at the cooler without touching it. "Did you happen to look inside?"

The boys exchanged guilty glances. Zoë braced herself.

"Well?"

"There was champagne," the older brother confessed. "Three full bottles. Nothing else. We, um…chilled them down and drank one last night. Maybe two."

Sean looked pained.

"We're sorry, Mr. Breeze," the younger brother rushed to say. "We will pay—"

"Good lord, no." Sean waved a hand. "Don't worry about that." His brows dipped. "Though you're a little young to be drinking, my boy."

Zoë stifled a smile at the face the kid made. "That stuff tasted awful. How can anyone like it?"

"Hang on to that thought," Sean said, rising and clapping the kid on the shoulder. "Now, who can show me on the chart exactly where you found the cooler?"

An hour later, cooler safely stowed aboard the *Summer Breeze*, they'd waved goodbye to the guys and made their way back through the reef, and were now heading south in pursuit of the first real clue they'd gotten to date.

"You think there'll be any fingerprints on the cooler?" Zoë asked Sean excitedly. She was sitting next to him in the passenger seat as he checked over the controls. She'd noticed how careful he'd been while bringing the cooler onboard.

"I doubt it," he said. "If the killer is smart enough to change jurisdictions between murders, he's probably not going to leave his prints lying around. To be honest, I'm starting to wonder if there is a connection. I mean, champagne?"

She put her chin in her hand. "Hmm. The Blantons

must have brought it with them when they rented the *Hasty Breeze*. Maybe this place we're going is where they met up with the killer. Somehow he lured them away and they forgot the cooler on the beach."

"But they were killed on Qamea. And by then they'd already told me they lost the yacht. As far as I know, they weren't with anyone else when I argued with them in that bar."

"Ho-kay, so much for that theory," she said wryly. "This is why I'm not a cop but a hotel evaluator."

"And a damn good one, too," he said, leaning over to give her a kiss on the nose.

Suddenly, she shot straight up in horror. "Good grief. My job! The Indigo's evaluation. The staff arrives today, don't they? I should be there!"

"What's the hurry?" he asked, his mouth thinning in displeasure. "You have the rest of the week to finish up, don't you?"

All at once the world seemed to close in on her, squeezing the breath from her lungs. *The rest of the week…* Then she'd be gone.

She dragged air back into them before she passed out.

"Yes," she managed to say. "I guess there's no rush."

"Good." There was a long pause, then he said, "Have you thought any more about what I asked you?"

The breath left her again. "Sean—"

He cut her off. "You wouldn't have to quit your job, Zoë. Your boss is my friend. I can tell him you want to live here, with me. It would be cheaper for the company if you were based out of Fiji anyway. Closer to Asia. Surely they must need evaluators there?"

She stared at him in a mire of indecision. Never had

she been so tempted in her life. To throw caution to the wind. To say *yes, yes, yes!* and damn the consequences.

Tempted. But not crazy.

"Breeze," she said, deliberately using his nickname. Reminding herself of the folly and the probable outcome. "I'm not even on the Secret Traveler's international team yet. My promotion depends on how well I do on this job. If I blow it, it's not going to matter if you're his friend."

He regarded her with an angry frown. "You're avoiding the real question."

"Yes," she said with a sigh. "I am."

And she had no intention of addressing it. The fact that he wanted sex and she wanted love was not a debate she wished to engage in. Lord. Nothing would make him run away faster. She didn't blame him. His ex-wife had burned him badly. But Zoë needed more. She needed real feelings, and some kind of commitment. She wasn't about to demand them of Sean. But she wasn't about to uproot her entire life for anything less.

But in the meantime, she could give him what he wanted.

"There are better ways to spend our days together than arguing," she said. And pulled at the strings of the maillot bathing suit he'd bought her. She peeled it down and off her body.

He watched her undress with a hooded, brooding gaze. But to her surprise, he made no move to touch her. He just looked. And looked.

"You are so damn beautiful," he said at last. Then he turned his eyes toward the deserted shore. "This is it. We're here."

"Don't."

Sean had gone aft to lower the dinghy as Zoë bent to pick up her maillot from the deck. After all, he was acting as though he hadn't even noticed she'd just tried to seduce him.

"Don't get dressed," he told her in a firm voice.

She had never been the adventurous type. Not before she'd met Sean. But she had to admit, she secretly enjoyed the wicked thrill, the titillating edge of danger, knowing at any moment a stranger might walk or sail past and catch her with no clothes on. Her naked dance in the waves the other night had been the most shockingly wanton thing she'd ever done in her life. And she'd loved every minute of it.

She smiled. "All right. But if someone shows up you're giving me your trunks."

"We'll see about that."

The lagoon George had marked on the chart was shallow, the reef lying close to shore, so they'd decided to anchor farther out and row in. The dinghy was cramped, with just a center bench, which Sean took so he could man the oars, and a small triangle seat in the bow for her. He'd tossed in some snorkel gear and a bottle of water, which lay at their feet.

He was still broody, miffed that she'd refused to talk further about their situation. And for once her being naked was not distracting him, even though he'd insisted on it.

She, on the other hand, took one look over the side at the teeming reef under the crystal clear turquoise water and forgot everything else.

"Oh, my God," she exclaimed. "Look at the coral. It's gorgeous!"

He grunted and kept rowing, barely sparing a glance at the wonderland below.

"Is that why you brought the gear? Could we go snorkling?"

"After we check out the beach."

"Right. Of course."

So she dutifully helped him examine the narrow strip of black sand beach for further evidence of the Blantons or the *Hasty Breeze*, but the intervening tides had washed the shore to a satin-smooth finish, and after a thorough search the only things they found besides seashells were two more empty champagne bottles thrown up into the jungle fringe.

"Well," she said, discouraged. "At least we know we're in the right place."

"I just wish I could figure out what the hell happened here."

She peered at him. "I don't think you need to be a cop to figure that one out."

He hiked a brow.

"A beautiful beach, a young couple, two bottles of champagne…?"

His brows dipped again. "Besides that."

"Speaking of which…" She put her arms around his neck. They weren't going to find anything, and she was tired of his dark mood. "You haven't kissed me for hours. I'm going through withdrawal."

"All you want me for is sex," he grumbled. But his hands slid down her ribs to her hips and pulled her close. His mouth covered hers and he kissed her long and hard. When they came up for air, he murmured with a mock sigh, "I'm starting to feel used."

She chuckled. He was also starting to feel aroused. "Yet you're the one who's keeping me naked and barefoot."

He gently thumbed her breast. "You objecting?"

"Mmm. Never. You?"

"Only to your leaving."

"Sean—"

"No, I won't stop saying it. I persuaded you to sleep with me. I'll talk you into staying, too. Wait and see."

She sighed and kissed him. "You're impossible, you know that?"

"Only when you cross me. Otherwise I'm pretty damn easy."

She smiled even though she wanted to beat her fists against his chest and tell him to stop it, just stop it. It was hard enough being in love with him knowing she had to leave soon, but to have him trying to talk her into staying, it was too much to bear. She had to be too strong. Too sensible. When her whole heart was crying out to be weak and impractical, if only it could have him to love forever!

But it was the whole forever thing that was stopping her. That *must* stop her. Because it was only a fantasy. She knew that. But resisting the urge to break down was hard. The hardest thing she'd ever done.

"You promised to take me snorkeling," she said,

pulling away, because if they made love right now she had the sinking feeling she'd totally give in to him and do whatever he asked.

"Stay close," Sean admonished her as they adjusted their masks and fins and flipped backward off the dinghy.

The reef was the strangest, most utterly amazing world Zoë'd ever been in. Under the glass-clear blue water, long, delicate fans of soft coral undulated in the gentle current in a rainbow of electric hues: oranges, reds, pinks, brilliant whites fringed with fluorescent purple.

Thousands of striped and metallic and neon-hued fish instantly surrounded them, flashing brilliantly as they danced in endless schools among the lace-like branches. Sean took her hand and guided her down stairways of flat table coral floating as though weightless above the shell-strewn bottom. They swam through secret grottos rimmed with long, mysterious waving fingers of red and squat, cabbage-like green formations, and explored deep canyons of stunningly vibrant hard corals curtained by forests of waving seaweed, teeming with yellow sea anemones, blue starfish and myriad fluttering, scooting, nibbling fish of every size and description.

They grinned at each other through their masks and held hands and chased and rolled each other round and round under the water until they were gasping for breath and laughing through their snorkels and she never, ever wanted to come up to the real world again.

Then suddenly, Sean grasped her around the waist,

his arm catching her in an iron grip, and turned her so she was looking away from him, paddling his swim fins so their heads stayed just below the surface and they could both breathe through their snorkels.

Then he pointed.

About a hundred feet away, and closing in fast, was a huge, gray shark.

Chapter 13

The shark was coming right at them!

Zoë's heart literally stopped, then took off into hyperspeed. Panic burst over her. She struggled to get away from Sean. But his arm was like a steel band around her waist. He didn't utter a sound. But the power of his will came through loud and clear, telegraphed from every taut muscle, every calm breath he took.

Stop struggling. I'll take care of you.

She managed to inhale a steadying breath and forced herself to relax in his embrace.

His free hand gave her two quick squeezes, then it was somehow holding his lethal black dive knife. He held it out in front of them as the gray beast glided closer and closer. She looked around for the dinghy, but by now it was on the other side of the shark. No rescue there. Despite that, Sean's heartbeat was slow and steady against her back, his breathing unhurried. He wasn't panicked at all....

She was. To her, the shark looked like a primordial death machine. A sickly shade of shiny green-gray with dull brown blotches on its back, it was bearing down on them with alarming speed. Its flat snout flared open, revealing a gaping mouth with rows of vicious, pointed teeth.

A scream clawed up her throat. Sean's grip tightened reassuringly. The shark hurtled through the water. *They were going to die!* She squeezed her eyes shut, expecting the rip of flesh and a painful death. Instead she felt the tingling rush of displaced water, the sweep of a massive, menacing presence as it turned at the last second and glided harmlessly past.

To her shock, Sean whooped in exhilaration, his laughter echoing through the snorkel. Her eyes popped open.

She couldn't believe it. The man was *enjoying* this!

In fact, his enjoyment was tangible, physical—thick, hard and long against her backside.

The shark swam in a wavy circle, sucking up an occasional fish as it cruised the reef, looking fat and thankfully well-fed. Then it headed back around toward them. That's when Sean pressed the knife handle into her palm.

She swallowed the taste of terror in her mouth, closing her eyes again and gripping the false security of the knife as the shark brushed past them in another near pass. She suddenly realized Sean's hands were on her bare breasts, squeezing them tight and rolling her nipples between his fingers. An adrenaline-burst of need combined with her fear and blazed through her center like an electric shock. She dropped the knife.

And let out a moan that was a hot, roiling keen. *Breathe!* she told herself, frantically sucking air through the snorkel, grateful he had enough control to keep their heads at the surface.

The shark turned on a dime and punched through the water back toward them.

Lightning-fast, Sean's grip moved to her thighs. He grasped and parted them, and in one scything thrust he slid deep into her. He was thick and pulsing with power, dangerous as the shark that toyed with them. She turned her head and met his storm blue eyes. They burned with excitement, mesmerizing her with their intensity and the depth of the pleasure that radiated from them as he plunged into her deeper still. Every molecule of her body felt thrillingly alive.

She turned back to the shark, faced it as it showed her its teeth, its nostrils flaring as it approached, watching them with its black, beady eyes. Her pulse beat out of control. Sean was huge and hard inside her, with one large hand enveloping her breast, squeezing and pinching. The shark came closer. Her heart beat faster, faster. Sean's other hand slid between her legs just as the shark slid past them, blowing a burst of cool water from its gills and grazing her leg with the tip of its horrible, leathery fin. She screamed. Sean touched her.

Her whole being convulsed as they burst through the surface and into the air, gasping and crying out as the orgasm tore through her like hot lava. He held her hips firmly against him and gave two remorseless thrusts and then he, too, called out in release. They splashed and rolled and shuddered together, and she was terrified she would either be eaten alive or drown, but she couldn't stop the relentless terror-pleasure that held her in its throes. Until the spasms subsided and she realized he was floating on his back on the surface with her in tow between his legs and the dinghy was dipping in the waves just a few yards away.

He disengaged and they both ripped off their masks at the same time.

"Are you in*sane*?" she demanded, peering nervously down into the water below.

"It's a sand tiger shark," he said. "They're curious but basically harmless."

She didn't know whether to laugh or cry or beat the crap out of him. "You could have told me!"

"And spoil the—"

But then he suddenly let out a curse and his eyes went wide, and she gasped, too, because it struck them both at exactly the same moment.

They'd forgotten to use protection.

Strangely, Sean felt no panic.

Stranger still, he felt pleased, almost triumphant.

"You'll *have* to stay now," he stated, helping her into the dinghy.

"Don't be ridiculous," she snapped. "I'm not pregnant."

"And you know this how?" he asked, amazingly calm considering this was the worst disaster he could have envisioned just a few short days ago. What the hell had happened to him since then?

"It's the wrong time of month. And besides, isn't salt water spermicidal?"

He had no idea, but he hoped she was wrong. He studied her body, so curvy and perfect. She'd look even more beautiful carrying his child. "Would it be so bad?"

She stared at him incredulously. "Sean. We've known each other for three days."

"Four," he corrected.

"You're deliberately missing the point."

She should know. "Which is?" he asked.

"That neither of us wants this. Neither of us is ready for this. We can't even agree on our own relationship, let alone dragging an innocent child into the picture."

Ouch.

"If you weren't so goddamn stubborn," he muttered, holding the ladder so she could climb up onto the *Summer Breeze*'s deck.

He jumped up after her and caught her around the waist. And realized her body was shaking. He wrapped his arms around her, concerned. "You're trembling. What's wrong, baby?"

"Gee, I can't imagine." Her breath hitched on a laugh that sounded almost desperate. "I've had a pretty intense morning. Give me a minute to equalize."

He scraped the hair from her face and gazed at her, filling with a bone-deep fear. She couldn't leave him now. She *couldn't*.

"I'm taking you home," he said. "Back to the Indigo Inn. We can talk about things later."

"But what about the killer? And the *Hasty Breeze*?"

"It can wait."

She seemed to rally. "No. If we don't find them Sanjit will arrest you."

He smiled. "So you do care."

"Oh, stop it." She hit him in the arm. But there was no heat behind it. "Seriously. We can't give up now."

"I have no intention of giving up. But things have changed. We should go back and—"

"Sean. Read my lips. Nothing's changed."

"*Everything's* changed. If you're pregnant—"

"I'm *not*," she interrupted and held up a hand to stop him speaking. "But okay, let's pretend for argument's sake I am. What are you trying to tell me?"

"That I want to take care of it. Of you. I want you to move here and—"

"Wait." She pressed the air with the hand she was still holding up. "Are you saying you're going to marry me?"

There was that word again. For a second he was paralyzed with a fear far worse than anything he'd ever felt confronting a whole bevy of sharks. He swallowed it down. "Yeah, I'll marry you if that's what it takes."

She regarded him, the strangest smile coming over her face. It looked more like pity than humor. "Gosh, and what girl could resist such a romantic proposal?"

She dropped her hand and shook her head, turning to walk away.

"Zoë!" He snagged her arm. "That's not fair. You know I didn't mean it like it came out."

"Yeah, you did," she said. "But that's okay. Really." She took a deep breath, her smile turning strong. Stronger than any smile he'd ever seen before. "Contrary to popular opinion, not every woman is pining away for a husband. Some of us have satisfying, fulfilling lives without one."

That, he didn't doubt. Why should women be different than men? "And if there's a child?" he asked.

Her eyes went soft. "Admittedly, that complicates things. But women do it every day."

He drew her reluctant body into his arms and held her. "I wouldn't let you do it alone. There's no way. You know that, right?"

She sighed. "Yes. I know. And I'd be so lucky to have you as the father of my child. You're a good man, Sean."

For some reason her words caused a burning knot of emotion to roil behind his eyes. It was the nicest thing anyone had ever said to him. Ever.

Swallowing heavily, he put his lips to her hair and held them there for a long moment. Until she said, "But I'm still not pregnant."

Yeah, well. They'd see about that.

He was having a hell of a time concentrating.

Sean jetted out a breath and swung the binoculars back to the far end of the last deep lagoon they needed to examine before turning the *Summer Breeze* around to continue their search on the other islands to the north and east of Taveuni. This was the third pass he'd started. But each time his thoughts had struck out on their own and he'd found himself staring into space instead of looking for the distinctive white hull and blue lettering of the *Hasty Breeze*. The trouble was, the closer they got to the popular dive areas of the southern tip of the island, the more boats they ran across, making the process of elimination more difficult.

Sure it was. Who was he kidding? He'd had no trouble yesterday searching the equally popular north-western bays and lagoons.

Sweet mercy.

Had he really said he'd marry her?

And had she really turned him down flat?

Now, that put a whole different spin on things, didn't it? Not that it should. But it did. Oh, yeah, it did.

Though for the life of him, he couldn't say why.

He pushed out another breath and gave up. "Thirsty?" he asked Zoë, who was lying on a towel on her stomach, elbow bent and chin propped in hand, a few feet away in the angled shade of the bimini. Her feet twirled lazily in the air above her pretty derrière.

"Sure, I'll have a beer," she said dreamily.

He got her a Fiji Water and dangled it in front of her. He could see the muscles in her jaw bunch. "Sean. I am *not* pregnant."

"Humor me."

"Fine." She looked up with an irritated smirk, then snatched his unopened beer from his hand and tossed it overboard.

"Hey!"

She made a face. "Humor me."

Resignedly, he watched his beer float away. "That's littering, you know."

"It'll probably make some castaway's day." She twisted the lid of her water and drank.

He clucked his tongue, reached into the cooler for another bottle of water, then changed his mind. Instead he grabbed a handful of ice. And smiled.

She let out a really satisfying screech when he

dropped a cube onto her backside. She flipped over with another yelp as the second cube dropped, and he grinned, ducking her water bottle as she flung it at his head.

"You are so getting it, Guthrie!"

"I'm counting on it, baby," he laughed, ice flying everywhere as she came at him. By the time he had her pinned down again, all the ice from the cooler was melting on the deck and they'd poured four ice-cold bottles of water all over each other. They were laughing hard as she was trying to wriggle away and they were both drenched, and he'd never wanted anyone more in his life, so he pulled down his trunks and caught her knees, spread them apart and dove into her.

They both gasped and the laughter slowly died but not the smiles, and they looked at each other as he adjusted and filled her to the hilt. They were both thinking the same thing, that he hadn't bothered with protection, and this time it was deliberate.

"It won't matter," she said softly. "You won't get me pregnant."

"How can you be so sure?" he stubbornly asked, while at the same time truly horrified with himself for even considering what he seemed to be doing with alacrity. He raised her knees and pushed in further. Determined.

"I know my body," she said, closing her eyes with a blissful smile as he withdrew and thrust in again. "My period. It'll be here in a couple of days. Three at the most. I can feel that."

Well, hell. His ex-wife had always gotten extra bitchy just before her time of the month. "Cramps?" he asked with a frown. "Headaches?"

"No, I never get any of that stuff, thank goodness."

"Then how?" he asked. "What do you get?"

She grinned up at him and said the best thing possible. "Extra horny."

Chapter 14

That night they made it back to Qamea. Scene of the crime.

Sean eased the *Summer Breeze* into a slip at the resort marina where he'd spent the night of the murders, waving to the attendant, Tiko, who'd be one of his principal witnesses if it came down to a trial against Sean.

Not that it would. He was feeling confident again. On the way here, they'd run into a group of guys fishing who'd told him they'd seen one of the *Breeze* boats a couple of days ago. They thought it had been over by Maruiti. Which just happened to be the small island Jeela's new husband, Wilson, hailed from. Now, admittedly, Sean did own seven yachts, all of which were christened some variation of *Breeze*, any one of which could be cruising these waters. But the coincidences just seemed to be piling up way too high. Disappearances, murders, abandoned coolers of champagne.

Something was going on with that boat.

Something that didn't add up.

He was absolutely certain all hell was just about to break loose. But as far as he was concerned, it couldn't come fast enough.

The first thing Sean did after they checked in at the swanky resort—which this time he insisted upon—was to get hold of a phone and call Inspector Sanjit with a report about the cooler they'd recovered from the missing yacht, which might have the killer's fingerprints on it.

Sanjit actually laughed. "What the hell do I want with some poor tourist's fingerprints?" he'd asked. "I know who murdered the Blantons. I have men out interviewing all your supposed witnesses. The ones we can find, anyway. Half of them are no longer in the country."

The man was a freaking dog with a bone. He'd diddle around until all the tourists went home, then discredit Sean's other witnesses, one by one, until the circumstantial house of cards was all that was left…just enough for a show-trial conviction. Sean knew how it worked.

If he could only get his hands on that damn boat, he might actually find some hard evidence to dispute the bastard.

Soon. He was so close he could taste it.

His second call was to Regi.

"Thank God, you rang," his lawyer exclaimed. "You aren't going to believe what I found out."

"Try me."

"The American Samoa murders, they were identical to the ones on Fiji."

"Ha! I knew it."

"Yes, yes," Regi said excitedly. "But there's more."

"Yeah?"

"More murders."

"What?"

"On a hunch, I put out feelers to other island countries around the Pacific. And one of my contacts came back with a tip. About another similar case."

"Seriously? Where?"

"Vanuatu."

Sean tried to remember where the heck that was. West of Fiji, as he recalled, about halfway to Australia.

"When did it happen?"

"Two weeks ago," Regi said. "Which puts it right between the other two incidents, timewise."

"And it's the same deal? A couple killed?"

"On the beach as they made love. Slashed horribly with a knife."

Sean drilled his fingers into his hair. "Unbelievable. Zoë was right. It really is a serial killer."

"Looks that way."

"Now all we have to do is convince the cops. Detective Inspector Sanjit, in particular."

Regi sniffed. "I already have a call in to his superior."

"For all the good it'll do."

"I think I'll also contact your FBI. They specialize in these things, don't they? Especially with an American territory and American citizens involved, surely they'll send someone to investigate right away. Let the officious twit just try and ignore the FBI."

Sean chuckled wryly. "Go get 'em, Regi."

"It's the least I can do. Indigo Bay wouldn't be the same with the Breeze behind bars."

"Tell me about it, my friend."

Suddenly, Sean spotted an all-too-familiar face among the crowd at the bar. *Tony. Again.* His eyes narrowed as suspicion attacked anew. "And Reg, listen, there's some American guy following me around. Can you find out who he is and what the hell he wants with me?" He gave him Tony's name and the few details he knew.

"Think he's working for Sanjit?"

"Can't imagine why else he'd be so interested in me. But an American? It makes me nervous. Shut him down if you can manage it."

"I'll see what I can do."

They chatted for a few more minutes then hung up.

"Any news?" Zoë asked, plopping down on the arm of his easy chair, holding a highball glass in her hand.

He grabbed it and sniffed it suspiciously, then took a swig. He wrinkled his nose. "Grapefruit juice?"

"With a dash of pomegranate. If you're going to be all over me like a bad rash about drinking, I may as well get some vitamins out of it."

Luckily, she didn't seem too broken up about being deprived. She put her arm casually around his shoulder, leaned over and kissed his temple. She was wearing another of the sexy dresses—well, gowns really—he'd bought for her the other day. It was the color of light purple orchids, long and sleek with a slit up one side and a neckline that showed exactly the right amount of her tempting cleavage—not too modest and not too revealing. The sapphire necklace nestled between her breasts.

"I don't care if it doesn't match," she'd declared as she'd gotten dressed earlier. "I'm wearing it every chance I get."

She'd said it with the slightest edge of wistfulness, almost as though she thought there wouldn't be many more chances. Which had made him tug her angrily to his chest and kiss her until she melted against him and then kiss her some more until, when he finally let up, she gazed up at him worshipfully, all thought of chances—and leaving—forgotten. That was more like it.

"Anyway, yes, there's news. Good news." He told her what Regi had said about the other crimes.

"Now Sanjit will have to admit he's wrong," she said with a warm smile and another kiss. "Does this mean we go back to the inn tomorrow?"

"I still want to find the *Hasty Breeze*. Why? You want to go back?"

Her eyes slid away, to the view out the window. *Uh-oh.* "I do need to finish my rating of the Indigo Inn soon," she said. "I report to my next evaluation site in just three days."

He ground his teeth. *He would not go ballistic.* He would *not* be unreasonable, and he would *definitely* not throw her over his shoulder and haul her back to the Indigo to handcuff her to his bed. No matter how much he wanted to.

"Okay," he forced himself to calmly say. "Give me

one more day. If we don't find the *Hasty* by tomorrow night, we'll head back home."

She caught her bottom lip between her teeth and nodded. Then she abruptly rose. "Come on," she said. Her voice cracked and she cleared her throat. "I'm starving. Let's eat."

That night they made love.

Really made love. For the first time.

In fact, it was the first time Sean had ever truly made love to any woman. Before tonight, he'd had no idea what it really meant, making love. He'd always thought of it as sex.

This was different.

Way different.

It scared the spit out of him.

But it was good. So incredibly good.

Zoë's body was warm and soft and giving as she moaned and sighed and whispered words of love into the crook of his throat that he was pretty sure she never intended him to hear because she couldn't possibly mean them. But he matched her words with his body. Showing her with his lips and his tongue and his cock all the things he wanted to say back to her. That he adored her. That he worshipped her. That he wished to hell he'd met her when he still had a heart that trusted, and a hope that love could work. He wished that more than anything. So it was probably a good thing she didn't mean those words of love, because a woman who really meant words like that deserved better than him. Far better. She deserved someone who could return that sweetly offered love wholeheartedly. Someone who wasn't terrified to throw himself off that bridge. Someone who'd enjoy the fall.

But making love he could do. He could revel in the physical, could throw himself into loving her body as well as any man could ever love a woman. And pray that it was enough for her. Enough to make her want to stay with him.

If she didn't stay, he didn't know what he'd do.

Because this was different. He never wanted it to end. Ever.

And that *really* scared the spit out of him.

The next morning they got an early start.

They'd both been restless after making love. They'd wrapped their arms around each other and spooned one way and then the other, then made love again, but nothing seemed to take the edge off the heavy, unspoken tension that hummed through the bed.

Their days were numbered, the end of the affair drawing near, and they both knew it.

Two days left. And two nights.

As they nestled together in a lounger on the deck of the *Summer Breeze* sipping coffee and watching the sun come up, they didn't speak. Good thing. Sean didn't think he could make small talk if his life depended on it. Zoë looked like she was barely holding it together. *Hormones,* he thought. He didn't care if she insisted she wasn't carrying his child. He didn't believe it. She was. She had to be.

His heart warmed, remembering the sweet praise she'd given him without a second thought. *I'd be so lucky to have you as the father of my child.*

No, *he'd* be the lucky one.

He kissed her and smiled wistfully, and she smiled bravely back.

"Ready?" he asked, just as the sun peeked over the horizon.

"Sure," she said, and took his empty cup. Then he went to strap on his knife and start the engine as she untied the lines. And they were off on the final day of their search for the missing yacht.

"Okay, *really* no freaking way," Sean muttered as they slowly putted into the half-moon bay that fronted the tiny village on the island of Maruiti. "This is too easy."

Zoë's hand slapped over her mouth, then met his disbelieving gaze with wide eyes.

There it was. The *Hasty Breeze*. Anchored and bobbing merrily in the middle of the lagoon as though it didn't have a care in the world. Which of course it didn't. *He* was the one with all the cares. Boats didn't have cares. Only idiot owners.

He tipped back his head and laughed.

"Jeela," he said at Zoë's look of astonishment. "She must have taken it when she eloped."

"Why on earth would she have done that?"

"Standing invitation. Any of the villagers are welcome to borrow my yachts if they aren't rented."

"But I thought it was? To the Blantons?"

"I'm sure we're about to get an earful of explanation," he said as he slipped on a shirt, pointing to the young couple waving enthusiastically at them from the deck.

Which, indeed, they did.

"Oh, I am so sorry, Mr. Breeze, I had no idea we caused so much trouble for you!" Jeela wailed after Sean gently explained what was going on. She looked genuinely stricken.

Her new husband, Wilson, appeared equally distressed. "I found the yacht moored in a hidden lagoon on the other side of our island. I saw a couple take the dinghy and leave. For two days they did not come back for it. I was sure the *Hasty Breeze* must belong to you, Mr. Breeze, so I thought I'd return it to you myself." His words faltered and he looked guiltily at his new wife.

"Go on."

"So I took it to your island…but I wanted to see Jeela first, and then—"

"It was my idea to use your boat to elope in before bringing it back to you, because you always say we can borrow your boats anytime," Jeela explained tearfully. "I'm so sorry!"

"I knew our forbidden marriage would cause problems," Wilson said, giving her a comforting hug, "but I never thought anyone would end up murdered, or accused of it!"

"That's not your fault," Zoë assured him. "None of that is your fault. You just wanted to be with the one you love. There's nothing wrong with wanting that."

Sean blinked, as did Wilson. Their eyes collided briefly and he gave the other man a nod. "That's right," he said, covering the young man's embarrassment. "This can all be straightened out. I'm just glad we found the *Hasty*, and that she's not a pile of kindling on some reef somewhere."

Wilson swiped his forehead. "We will go straight to

the police station in Savusavu and make things right for you. And return the boat to the marina, of course."

"Not necessary," Sean said with a dismissive gesture. "Seriously. Nothing you can say will make a difference to Sanjit anyway."

When Jeela went to protest, he shook his head. "It's okay. Regi has called in the FBI. They'll straighten him out. Meanwhile, I'll trade you for the *Summer Breeze*, and you can keep her as long as you like. Zoë and I will take the *Hasty* back to the Indigo and wait for the FBI to examine her."

"Are you sure?" Jeela asked, obviously still upset. "You are so generous, Mr. Breeze. What can we do to repay you?"

He glanced at Zoë. "Just make it right with your uncle and the village. He loves you very much but he's still the chief and his position has been affected. Perhaps it's time to stop this meaningless feud between the islands. Give it a try."

Zoë smiled as Jeela gave him a big hug and Wilson shook his hand, vowing to do what they could.

"You should be chief," Zoë told him with pride in her voice, later, after they'd all packed up their things and switched boats, and were now sitting at an impromptu feast thrown for them by the Maruiti chief, who just happened to be Wilson's uncle. Sean had immediately seen the possibilities, and after being honored in the *yaqona* ceremony again, started to help Wilson plant the idea of ending the feud between the islands.

"Nah. Maybe ambassador," Sean said with a grin. "More fun and less responsibility than chief. And you get to dress up."

Zoë gave him a crooked smile. "Ambassador Breeze. There's a certain ring to it."

The muscles of his forehead twitched. It was weird how quickly he'd gotten used to being called Sean again. And how completely wrong it sounded when she called him by the nickname everyone else used.

"Sean," he corrected. "Ambassador Sean."

The smile bent slightly. "No." She shook her head. "Chief Sean. Ambassador Breeze."

He was about to ask her what she meant by that, when the *derua* drums suddenly took up and began to beat out the distinctive rhythms of a woman's dance. The dancers ran in from the side and all conversation stopped as the village *daunivucu* singer began his epic chant. Which coincidentally, happened to be about a princess who was kidnapped by a rival island prince, thus starting a long and bloody feud between the islands. The crowd got a little rowdy during the middle, but by the surprisingly conciliatory ending, everyone was smiling and nodding at the story-chief's wise decision not to go to war.

Sean had a feeling the real-life island feud was finally about to come to an end. He only wished his and Zoë's seemingly insurmountable differences could be as easily resolved. He thought about it, and wondered if he hadn't been locked for all this time in his own feud—with the memory of his ex-wife. Perhaps it was time to let that go, too.

The sun was still a good bit above the horizon when they finally made their way to the *Hasty Breeze* and weighed anchor for home.

It had been a hell of a journey. Both literally and figuratively.

Was he the same person as when it had started? God no. What exactly had changed about him in the space of those few days spent with Zoë?

Hell, what hadn't? His whole attitude. Where he wanted to be, what he wanted to get out of life, how he wanted to live it. And with whom. Or at least…the possibility of sharing his life and love with another person. That was new. Perhaps he had already let that feud go….

Because of Zoë.

And if he was lucky, the journey wasn't over yet. If he had anything to say about it, it wouldn't end anytime soon.

He must get his hands on one of those home pregnancy tests. That would go a long way to convincing her to stay.

"Have you seen my sunglasses?" she asked, coming up from below. "I can't seem to find them."

He glanced around the helm and spotted the silver frames glinting on the deck by the cooler. "Yep. Here they are." He reached down for them.

All at once, an instrument on the panel just above him exploded.

"What the—" He ducked and covered his face with an arm as another one below it shattered, raining more bits of glass over him. To his horror, he saw that round holes punctured the dials.

My God!

"Down!" he shouted at Zoë, as he hunched behind the captain's chair and waved frantically at her. "Get back in the cabin!"

She halted uncertainly. "What's going on?"

"Someone's shooting at us!"

Chapter 15

Zoë's heart slammed into double-time. "Why would anyone be shooting at us?" she shouted up to Sean after hurtling back down the ladder.

She heard another glass disc explode. Sean swore a blue streak. "God *damn* it. If they hit one of the navigational instruments we're done for. Hang on!"

She grabbed the banister and listened, even more terrified because she was unable to see what was happening on deck. The boat turned violently, then lurched into running speed.

Behind her something else splintered. She yelped, determined not to scream, and scanned the salon.

"You okay?"

"They hit a porthole!"

"I'm not seeing a boat. The bastard must be on the island. The good news is he can't follow us."

Thank God. "I'm coming up."

"No! Stay where you—"

Like that was going to happen. She shot up the ladder and crouch-ran over to where Sean was kneeling between the captain's chair and the mangled instrument panel, steering almost blind in a zigzag pattern.

"Damn it, Zoë! He must have a rifle. We could still be in range!"

"Where is he?" she asked, carefully peeking out from their hiding place to search the island receding behind them. Her pulse was thundering so hard she could barely focus.

After a grim scowl, Sean pointed to the mouth of an inlet a mile or so from the lagoon where they'd been anchored. "Seemed like somewhere around there."

"You think it's the same guy? The killer?"

He pushed out a breath. "Fifteen minutes ago I would have said no. That the disappearance of the *Hasty* had nothing to do with the murder of the Blantons. Now I'm back to not being so sure."

He took the boat through a few more zigzags from his knees, then cautiously moved up to sit hunched on the captain's chair. "We should be far enough out now, but stay under cover for a few more minutes, just to be sure."

She didn't argue, but curled up obligingly at his feet. She wanted to be close to him, not in danger. "If it's not the killer, who could it be?"

"Obviously someone who doesn't want us to take the *Hasty*." He glanced down at her. "Unless there's something you haven't been telling me?"

She gave him a wobbly withering look. "Jealous husband, you mean?"

"Or boyfriend." One corner of his lip quirked. "He *was* shooting at me."

"Sure you haven't stepped on any toes lately? Maybe someone else's jealous husband?"

"Funny."

She wrapped her arms around his leg, comforted by his presence. He was so brave, and sure of himself. Slowly, her pulse returned almost to normal.

"So who could be so interested in the *Hasty Breeze*? And why?" she asked. "And why shoot at us, and not Jeela and Wilson? Not that I'd want that," she added hastily.

"Jeela and Wilson were staying put. Maybe they were planning to steal the yacht and we beat them to it."

"Makes sense."

"Remember Jeela and her husband's explanation? Something about it puzzled me."

"What was that?"

"Why would the Blantons abandon the *Hasty Breeze* but tell me she was lost?"

"They got tired of cruising around deserted islands? Wanted to go party a little and didn't want the bother of returning the boat?"

He looked doubtful. "I suppose it's possible."

"Or they could have left it for someone else to pick up. For instance, whoever is shooting at us."

"More likely." He looked grim. "Which would tell us…"

"The person shooting is probably not the killer?"

He looked even grimmer. "Unless the Blantons knew their killer."

After a quick glance backward, Sean straightened up and turned the speeding boat toward the open water. "This is way too convoluted. There's a piece missing that we're not getting. I guess we'll just have to let the professionals solve the case."

"Sanjit? You seriously think he'll do anything? Even about the shooting?"

"Doubtful. But it doesn't matter. Regi says the FBI will be here tomorrow. Let them deal with it. I just want to get you the hell away from this psycho."

"My hero." She laid her head on his knee, her fear trickling away completely. Knowing he was there for her, that she was his number one concern, warmed her as nothing else could. When had that ever happened before? Certainly not with a man. Even her father. He was more worried about the farm than anything else—including his wife and daughter. Although she'd always convinced herself it was *because* of his wife and daughter, so he could provide for them, that he'd been so consumed with work. But it didn't much matter. The result was the same.

With Sean it was different. He definitely seemed driven as well. But it was clear he cared about everyone around him. He *made* it clear.

Abundantly clear. That he cared about *everyone*. Not just one person. Not just her. She had to remember that. He wasn't treating her any differently than he treated everyone else in his life.

Except maybe the sex part.

Which was fine. She was fine with that. She had her career to think of. Who needed a man who was perfect in every way?

Except maybe the commitment part.

She sighed.

"You okay down there?"

"Yep," she said. "Guess it's okay to stand up now?"

"Not an assassin in sight."

She stood and eased nervously into the passenger chair, checking the sea all around the boat for any sign of trouble. Nothing. Except for the trouble *in* the boat. Sitting in the captain's chair.

She sighed again.

She was so beyond help.

Zoë thought they'd go straight back home, but Sean decided to take the *Hasty Breeze* to Savusavu to report the shooting. And appeal to Sanjit to order a forensic examination of the yacht, in anticipation of the FBI special agent's arrival.

No such luck. They were told curtly by the desk officer that Inspector Sanjit was no longer involved in the case and had returned to headquarters in the capitol. No one here at the station was authorized to order forensics for that case. The shooting? Here, fill in this form. Have a nice day.

"Great. Now the cops are actually working *against* justice," Sean grumbled after they left the station.

"We could wait for the FBI to show up," Zoë suggested, even though the thought of Sean's massive bed back home was incredibly appealing. "Spend the night here at the marina."

Sean thought about it for a minute, then shook his head. "No. The FBI don't know about the developments with the yacht. They'll be looking for me at the Indigo. We should go there."

By the time the *Hasty* cruised into Indigo Bay it was several hours after dark. Nevertheless, there was a smiling boy who met them at the dock and took the lines to secure the boat, and a young man who hurried down to carry their things up to the boathouse, including the mound of gold boxes with all Sean's gifts. The sapphire necklace was still around her neck. She couldn't bear to take it off.

The inn itself was a bevy of activity compared to the days she'd spent here earlier that week. Two couples lounged with drinks on the verandah chatting about the charming pair of colorful red-and-green parrots that preened above them for handouts, another two couples were having coffee and dessert in the salon, and Zoë had noticed a man and woman walking hand-in-hand along the beach when they'd arrived.

"We're completely full," Aruna declared enthusiastically, meeting them in the great room. "We had a last-minute inquiry so I gave them Miss Zoë's room as you instructed, Mr. Breeze."

Zoë couldn't help blushing just a little. It wasn't like it hadn't been perfectly obvious she'd slept with Sean her only night at the Indigo. The unmade bed in her room and her dashing off to bail him out of jail would have been dead giveaways. Still. Embarrassing. Especially since it was painfully obvious there were no plans for her to stay.

"Excellent. Any crises to sort out?" Sean asked the hostess.

"Nothing I can't handle," she said with a grin.

"You're a lifesaver, Aruna. Remind me to give you a raise."

Her grin broadened as she straightened her apron and headed back off to the kitchen. "Oh, I will, Mr. Breeze. I will, indeed."

"What should we do now?" Zoë asked after the cheerful hostess disappeared. "Call Regi? The FBI?"

"First things first. We greet our guests," he answered, visually shifting gears, raking back his wind-blown hair, plastering a welcoming smile onto his sun-chapped lips—or were they kiss-chapped? Anyway, gone was Sean the worried man, replaced by Breeze the genial host. It was amazing how he did that.

So for the next hour they went around and Sean introduced himself and Zoë to the inn's guests. He still presented her as his "friend," but kept his arm slung possessively around her shoulders, occasionally giving her kisses on the hair as they chatted. When the first couple asked with knowing looks when she planned to move to Fiji, she brushed off Sean's, "Yeah, I'm still working on that," with a laugh. But by the time the fifth couple asked the same question, and he'd upped the ante each time so now it was, "I keep asking but she's determined to torture me by not answering," she was totally flustered.

The man was using extortion to get his way!

"You're being unfair," she scolded under her breath as he gave her another kiss, a real one this time.

"How? Because I want my lover with me? And my baby?" he added in a whisper for her ears only.

"There's no baby," she repeated again after they'd finally said their good nights and were strolling back to the boathouse. She was starting to feel like a broken record.

"Prove it," he said.

"I will. Any day now."

"And if not, you'll stay."

"Sean—"

"Breeze!"

They looked up to see a man trotting up the jetty toward them, after having handed over a small motorboat to the attendant. It was Regi. And he was smiling. Sort of.

"Hey, Reg! What's up?" Sean shook his hand with a masculine slap.

"I heard you two were back. Wanted to give you an update in person."

"Come on up for a drink," Sean said.

Regi waved him off. "Sorry, no time. Just stopping on my way home." He handed Sean a newspaper. "Check it out."

She watched curiously as he unfolded it. His eyes immediately widened. "Holy crap." He held it up for her to see.

The headline splashed across the entire top in huge black letters.

Sex-on-the-Beach Killer Loose in Fiji!

Zoë's jaw dropped. "Sex-on-the-Beach Killer?"

"Quaint moniker, eh?" Regi said, shaking his head. "The press can always be counted on to come up with the most sensational nickname for the most horrendous criminals."

"That is so sick."

"The story broke this morning. Front page on Fiji,

American Samoa and Vanuatu. By evening we'd heard from three other islands with possibly linked crimes."

"You are kidding," Sean said. "Three more? With couples on the beach and everything?"

"Well, from the evidence it appears likely only one, from two months ago on Tonga, is really the same guy."

"Jeez. Even so, that makes four incidents. *Eight* people murdered. My God, how could this have gone unnoticed?"

Regi shrugged philosophically. "Different countries. Different jurisdictions. No computers. If it weren't for you trying to clear yourself, the connection may never have been discovered."

"That's insane," Zoë said, appalled.

Again Regi shrugged. "Much of the South Seas' appeal to tourists is that it's like stepping back in time. But living in the past has its downsides, too. This is one of them."

"Maybe these crimes will help change that particular aspect."

He smiled. "Perhaps."

"Did you ever find out anything about our bad penny, Tony?" Sean asked.

"I'm afraid not. He's a hard man to trace. Not in any of the usual databases. Could he be using a false name?"

"I guess he must be. I may just have to ask him next time he shows up."

"Be careful, Breeze. A man with no name is usually a dangerous man."

"I will. Thanks."

A few minutes later they waved to Regi as he pulled his small speedboat away from the dock. Sean's gaze kept straying to the *Hasty Breeze*, moored on the other side of the dock.

"What are you thinking?" she asked him.

He pushed out a breath. "I was so looking forward to spending the night in my own bed." He turned and gave her temple a kiss. "With you."

She tipped her lips up to brush his again. "So was I. What's changed?"

Looping his arms around her waist, he laid his forehead against hers. She could feel the tension in his muscles as he spoke. "You heard what Regi said. This sex-on-the-beach guy is crazy. He needs to be stopped. So if there's even the smallest chance of evidence of his identity being on the *Hasty*, I have to make sure it's not compromised before the FBI can examine her. By guarding her tonight."

Alarm zinged through Zoë's insides. "But that might not be safe. What if it really was this madman shooting at us? What if he's followed us here?"

"Exactly why I need to make sure he can't get on-board and destroy evidence."

She grasped Sean's arms, suddenly frightened. Really frightened. The guy had tried to kill them already. "That's the police's job. You could be killed!"

"Baby, the police don't want to know. That's why I have to do it myself. I'm not letting this guy get away if I can possibly do something to stop him."

Despite the panic flooding her body, she knew what she must do. She took a deep breath. "In that case, I'll help."

His body went rigid and he shook his head. "Zoë, no—"

She laid a silencing finger over his mouth. "Save your breath, Sean. I'm staying with you."

His lips pressed into a thin line under her finger. "No."

She took his face between her hands and kissed those unyielding lips. "And how are you planning to stop me?"

"I'll tie you to my bed if I have to."

Though trembling inside, she smiled. "Why don't we save that until after the FBI leaves?"

He blinked. His mouth opened and closed. "If you're trying to distract me—"

"Working, isn't it?"

A muscle jumped in his cheek, then abruptly he went all businesslike again. "No. Zoë, he *kills* people. Couples. Like us."

She felt a brief flutter in her heart. "Only while they're making love. We just have to resist the temptation, that's all."

He muttered a curse.

"Meanwhile you could send one of your people out to do some night fishing in the bay. With a walkie-talkie."

He jetted out a long, even breath. She knew she had him. "You're more stubborn than a mule, you know that?"

"So I've been told. Well?"

He literally growled. "I don't like it. I don't like it one damn bit. If anything happens to you, I'll—"

"Nothing's going to happen. Do you own a gun?"

"No!" There was a pause before he added, "But I do have a couple of spear guns."

She smiled. "Those will do."

* * *

In order not to destroy any more evidence onboard, they decided to haul a couple of padded lounge chairs down from the boathouse's verandah along with some light blankets, and set up watch on the dock next to the *Hasty Breeze*.

To the Indigo's young night bellman's delight, he was dispatched in a small aluminum boat to fish at the mouth of the bay for the night, with instructions to call in to Mr. Breeze if any vessel ventured into Indigo Bay waters. Aruna promised to send down fresh coffee from the inn every hour. Even Rhett and Scarlett flew down from their usual night perches to flap around over the yacht, chattering like monkeys, finally landing and settling down with a preening of colorful wings on the bimini frame.

The moon hadn't risen yet, and only the spangling of stars overhead lit the bay, their reflections sparkling in the ever-moving sea. The teasing scents of salt and jungle flowers blended in the warm summer air in an exotic fragrance no Paris *parfumerie* could ever hope to duplicate. If they weren't keeping watch for a serial killer, it would be amazingly romantic.

"Do you really think he'll show up?" Zoë asked, scanning the horizon nervously.

"No. Not really," Sean answered, his voice calm and soothing in the darkness, despite the fact that she'd seen him strap on his dive knife—something she'd never seen him do at home before. "With that headline I think he's halfway to China by now."

"So all that arguing was for…what?"

He rolled his head to look at her. "You really have to ask?"

She sighed, torn between irritation and warm fuzzies. "No. I guess not." She didn't know how she felt about being the object of his protectiveness, and his desire, while still falling short of his love.

No. She did know. It felt like there was a huge black hole in her heart.

"Anyway," she said quietly. "It'll soon be over."

His expression didn't change. He just continued to regard her steadily. The endless canopy of stars shone back at her from the fathomless depths of his eyes.

God, she loved him so much.

Life was so unfair.

She was also so exhausted, from the roller-coaster week of emotional and physical excesses, that even Aruna's coffee couldn't keep her awake.

She slept. An uneasy sleep, filled with dreams of sharks and killers and blood and spear guns and a Sean so angry he sounded like a pirate threatening to make someone walk the plank.

"Just wait. You'll taste the brine of Davey Jones's locker yet, you obnoxious little bastard," he muttered in a low, pirate-gravelly voice, then laughed sinisterly.

Zoë forced her leaden lids up, shielding her sleep-sensitive eyes from the sun that hovered just above the horizon. Her pulse took off at a gallop. Was he talking to the serial killer?

An unholy yapping came from the direction of the yacht. Scarlett and Rhett flapped their wings and howled like banshees.

Good grief. Just the parrots doing their usual obnoxious animal imitations and wanting breakfast. She let out a breath of relief, swinging around to say good morning to Sean, but the words stuck in her throat.

He was sitting there holding a spear gun. Muttering, and aiming it right at the innocent birds.

"Hey!" she shouted, bounding off her lounger. She knocked the spear gun's aim down. Startled, he jumped up, hitting the trigger. The spear sang through the air. It sliced into one of the boat's dangling cushion fenders with a rip of plastic, then sank into the *Hasty's* hull with a loud thwack.

"What the hell!" he yelled in stunned surprise.

"You were going to shoot Rhett!" she accused.

"I was not!"

"I heard you threaten him! Both of them!"

"Of course I threatened them! They annoy the crap out of me every morning with their stupid barking and roaring and screeching, so I make empty threats to kill them in creative ways. That's what we do! It's a game. I'd never actually go through with it. Jeez, Zoë. How could you think that?"

Somewhere along the line her mouth had dropped open. She snapped it shut. "Well, how was I supposed to know?"

"I believe I've done it once or twice in front of you." He looked genuinely wounded.

Chagrined, she looked over at the spear sticking out of the Hasty's hull. She winced. Oops. But then she noticed something odd. Really odd.

"What's that?" she asked, staring at the stuffing that was coming out of the slice in the fender the spear had gone through. Except it wasn't stuffing. It was some

kind of paper. Colorful, rectangular bits of paper.
Sliding out of the gash and landing on the surface of
the water.

Floating there, it looked like…

It *was!*

Money!

Chapter 16

"Well, this explains why someone would want to get their hands on the *Hasty Breeze* so badly," Sean said, still reeling from the sight of so much cash. There were scores of bundles piled on the wooden boards of the dock, all taken from where they had been hidden in the dozen soft, elliptical hanging fenders that protected the boat from scraping against the dock. American dollars and euros. It had to be hundreds of thousands. Or even millions. "And why someone shot at us when we took the boat before they could get to it."

"Where did all this money *come* from?" Zoë asked, standing next to him, arms crossed over her abdomen and looking just as flabbergasted as he was. Even the parrots sitting on the bimini frame had gone reverently silent.

"Drug money would be my guess. Or some kind of heavy-duty smuggling." Both options were pretty common in these parts. Deserted islands had a habit of attracting pirates and other bad guys. Fiji had about three hundred uninhabited islands.

"Jeela and her husband?" she ventured.

"God, no. Impossible."

"The Blantons, then?"

He nodded. "Had to be them."

"And this is why they were killed, you think?"

"Makes sense. Deal gone wrong. Double-cross. Something. Although…"

She looked up. "What?"

"Why the other killings? That *doesn't* make sense."

"Good point." Her gaze shifted behind him to the bay. "Maybe the FBI will have an answer. Is this them?"

He whipped around and peered closely at the large official-looking craft cruising toward the marina. There was a guy in uniform at the helm and a man wearing a suit standing forward on deck. Who else but a feeb would wear a suit in hot, humid South Seas weather? Sean rolled his eyes, but was inwardly relieved.

"Looks like the cavalry," he said, and they walked over to help with the lines.

The suit made a practiced jump from the boat to the dock. Sean frowned. Something about the picture struck him as wrong. But he didn't get a chance to ponder it. The man strode briskly over to him and stuck out his hand.

"Hi. Agent Ford. You must be Guthrie."

"Yeah. Glad you're here," Sean said. Didn't the FBI call themselves *special* agents?

Ford darted a glance at the bundles of money piled on the deck. "Looks like I hit the jackpot." He homed in on Zoë, hand extended. His jacket flapped open, revealing a gun in a shoulder holster. "Hi. Agent Ford."

Sean suddenly noticed the uniform from the helm had also jumped onto the jetty, along with another man he hadn't seen before. Neither looked Fijian. Or American. A warning bell screamed to life in Sean's head.

"Zoë! Don't—"

Too late.

As she shook Ford's hand he yanked hard and she landed against his chest and he spun her around, his gun in the other hand, its barrel pressed to her head. Sean searched frantically for his second spear gun, but it was too far away.

"Don't move," Ford barked. "Or she's dead."

He froze. Hands out, palms up. "Okay. I'm not moving. Let her go."

Ford laughed. "Not likely." He jerked his head at the money. "Get it," he ordered the other men, who were joined by a third from the boat, who carried an assault rifle and stood guard, scanning the whole area all the way up to the inn. Sean prayed hard that Aruna had already arrived and wouldn't come walking down the path.

It took the two men about thirty seconds to load all the money into a couple of black garbage bags, tie and heave them up onto the deck of their cruiser.

"What are we going to do with these two?" one of the goons asked, jerking a thumb at Sean and Zoë.

The guard raised his rifle and snickered. "I vote for target practice."

"Yeah, you did so well on Maruiti," Ford said sarcastically.

"We could strip them naked and slash their throats, like the Sex-on-the-Beach Killer," one of the other guys said with an evil grin, pulling out a long knife. "After having a little fun first, of course."

Zoë gasped softly.

Sean clenched his teeth to keep from saying something that would get him killed.

Ford waved Knife Guy off. "That would only solve one of our problems. We can't risk being linked to the Blantons, since the morons went and got themselves killed. God knows what evidence they left behind on the yacht. It must be destroyed. Why not do both at the same time?"

"Ahh." The man next to Knife Guy slowly smiled. "Ka-boom," he said in a low voice, flaring his hands out dramatically.

"No!" Zoë protested. "You—"

Ford jammed the gun harder into her temple. "Shut up." He gestured to the other men. "Tape them up and get them onboard."

Zoë's scream was immediately cut off by Ford's hand over her mouth.

They weren't so gentle with Sean. His shouts never got past his throat because two men grabbed him by the arms while the other jerked his head back violently. Something vile was stuck into his mouth, then duct tape was slapped over it and wound around his head before he could utter a sound.

These guys had obviously done this before.

Sean had never been much of a praying man, but

now he got busy. Apparently someone up there was listening, because the scumbags didn't search him before taping his hands behind his back. His lower arm pressed against his dive knife, pushing it farther up under his shirttail. For all the good a knife would do against four men with automatic weapons. Even if he could pull it out, that would surely land him in a rain of bullets.

His and Zoë's wrists were taped and they were manhandled over onto the *Hasty*'s deck. She was crying. Her silent sobs ripped at his heart like razor blades. He would not let her die. He would *not*.

As they were shoved to the deck, he caught her eyes for a split second. Red and tear-drenched, they radiated fear and sorrow…and love. The look of pure love she gave him would have brought him to his knees if he weren't already there.

In that instant he knew he would do anything in the world to save her. To have her with him, keep her safe and happy. To love her for the rest of his life.

He wanted to shout and roar out his fury, and his frustration at not being able to tell her. Just tell her how much he loved her. How stupid he'd been not to say it while he'd still had the chance!

They were shoved down, wrenched around back to back, and ankles taped while more tape was wound around their torsos, binding them together. They sat with bodies bound to each other, possibly to die together, yet unable to communicate. He only hoped she'd seen his feelings written in his eyes, as he had in hers.

He was so preoccupied thinking about Zoë that it

came as a shock when the engines started and the *Hasty* shot forward away from the dock. Damn. What now?

It became all too clear what they had in mind when Ford tossed a coil of thin hemp rope across from the other boat, which was moving in tandem with them. Ka-boom Guy caught it and trotted aft to where the *Hasty*'s gas tank was located.

Double-damn.

Against his back, Zoë was shaking, sniffing back her tears. Their wrists had been taped together as well, sand-wiched between their spines. But because of that position, it was possible for him to grab her hand. He grasped her fingers tightly. She whimpered and grabbed him back.

"Mmphoy." He said her name, but with the tape and the gag in his mouth, the word came out like garbled oatmeal, as did his stab at encouragement, *Stay calm. We can do this.*

She stuttered out another whimper mixed with a sob. He squeezed her hand again. And watched with dread as Ka-boom Guy unlatched the cover to the gas tank intake and unscrewed the cap. He then threaded the rope partway down into the tank so about a meter was left outside as a fuse, laying it carefully on the deck like a deadly snake with its head in the tank.

He noticed Sean watching him, and grinned as he took a cigarette lighter out of his pocket. "Should give you about three minutes to contemplate eternity before the flame hits the gas. After that—" He snickered. "Like I said. Ka-*boom*."

All too quickly, the *Hasty* skimmed out of the bay and into the open sea, with the big cruiser at her side. The man at the helm brought her to a halt.

Ka-boom flicked his lighter.

Zoë screamed beneath her gag.

Sean's heart stopped.

The end of the rope was lit and the two men leaped off the *Hasty* onto the cruiser. In the blink of an eye the other vessel tore off, leaving a trail of foaming white water in its wake. None of the men even looked back.

Sean's heart started up again with a lurch. No time to lose.

"Mmphoy!" *Zoë!*

But she wasn't listening. She was yanking hard at their bonds trying to get loose. But she'd never be able to do it. He had to get to the knife at his waist but with her jerking his wrists around that wasn't possible.

"Mmphoy!"

She paused in her struggles. He squeezed her hand, let go and reached for his knife.

He couldn't get to it. His hands were turned the wrong way.

He glanced over at the rope fuse. About six inches had been burned.

He cursed violently. She started jerking at her bonds again.

"Hmmopc!" he yelled. *Stop!*

Miraculously, she did, turning her head to try and look at him. He turned, too. Their eyes met. The terror in her liquid blue eyes was killing him. He pleaded with her silently to be brave. She let out a muffled sob. He swallowed. Tried for the knife again. Couldn't reach it. *Damn!*

He checked the rope. A foot gone.

He had to get her to do it. Her hands were turned the right way to grasp it. She could do it. She had to! But she was too filled with fear to realize what he was doing. He had to get her to understand. Somehow.

"Mmphoy."

She gazed at him, glistening tears sliding down her cheeks. "Hmmp."

Suddenly an idea came to him. He cleared his throat. And started to hum a tune he hoped to hell she knew.

"Mack The Knife."

Zoë swallowed a sob of desperation.

The man was humming.

They were about to be blown to smithereens and the man was *humming!* And it wasn't even a love song.

She gave in to a final scream of anguish.

This was it. They were going to die.

"Mmphoy!"

She sucked in a deep breath through her nose, blocking out the dismaying smell of burning hemp, and turned her head again to face him. His eyes locked onto hers like lasers. He scowled fiercely. Grabbed her hands. And started to hum again.

While he hummed, he awkwardly raised their hands up and to her left. It suddenly hit her. He was trying to tell her something.

What?

She forced herself to concentrate. He nodded firmly, apparently seeing the dawning in her eyes. And kept humming.

The tune. It sounded vaguely familiar. Old.

Omigod! "Mack the Knife!" *Knife!* How could she have forgotten? She nodded excitedly. *Omigod, omigod, omigod.*

Quickly she yanked their hands over to his hip, groping around for it.

There!

Though her fingers were shaking badly, she managed to unsnap its sheath and slide it out.

Now what?

But before she could decide, he'd taken the blade from her and was busy slicing through the duct tape binding his wrists. He gave a sharp grunt, and something warm and wet oozed over her fingers. He'd cut himself.

"Mfhmmn!" she cried.

Suddenly his hands were free. A few seconds later he'd cut the tape from his mouth.

"Thank God," he murmured, spitting out the rag they'd stuffed in his mouth. "Hang on, baby. We'll get out of this."

She glanced desperately at the rope. Only about a foot left. "Mfhmmn, hhmmy!"

He leaned away from her back and a moment later his fingers were fumbling with her wrists. "Damn it, I don't want to cut you."

"Hndnnfkhmm!"

"Right." She felt the tape give. "No time for more, let's go." He swept her up into his arms and ran for the opening in the rail as she tore the tape from her skin, freeing her wrists. "Take a big breath, Zoë. I'll cut the rest in the water."

They sailed out over the side. She closed her eyes, took a huge breath and tried not to scream. Somehow her hands found their way around his neck and he let go of her legs before they hit the water. They shot down deep below the surface, clinging to each other. Underwater, he banded an arm around her waist and swam hell bent for leather away from the yacht.

Her lungs burned and the sea pressed in on her like a vise. The gag was still in place and salty water was leaking past it into her mouth, trying to trickle into her lungs. She couldn't swim because her ankles were still taped.

Panic welled like a mushroom cloud within her. She needed to breathe! Sean put his arms around her and headed for the surface. She forced herself to stay calm and trust him.

They broke surface and she dragged in a lungful of precious air. Instantly, Sean dove down again and sliced her ankles free so she could tread water.

"Come on, keep going!" he shouted as soon as he surfaced again. They swam like crazy, putting more distance between them and the yacht.

A loud sizzling noise gave them an instant's warning. Sean grabbed her shoulders and pushed her below the surface just as a huge explosion ripped through the air. The shock wave hit them like a body punch.

A hailstorm of debris hit the water around them, including spots of burning fuel. But a few moments later it was calm enough they were able to pop their heads above water for a quick, much-needed breath.

A million bits of wood and fiberglass that had once been the *Hasty Breeze* coated the surface like so much confetti, bigger chunks sinking down through the water past them like a slow-motion rain. A couple hundred meters away, the burning hulk of what was left of the vessel tipped to one side and slowly sank.

Sean turned her away from the awful sight and held her face still as they treaded water and he cut her gag. After sheathing the knife, he gently peeled the tape back from her mouth.

And then he kissed her. It was the best, most wonderful kiss she'd ever experienced in her life. And he was the best, most wonderful man in the world. And to think she'd almost lost him.

"Oh, God, Sean," she cried softly. "I thought we were dead for sure."

"So did I, sweetheart." He tenderly scraped a lock of wet hair from her cheek. That's when she noticed the blood oozing from a long cut on his wrist.

"You're hurt!" She grasped his hand and examined the wound. It was bleeding, but didn't appear to be too deep.

"I'll live," he said, glancing around. "We'd better start swimming. In case they decide to come back."

She followed his gaze to the silhouette of the big cruiser that was thankfully growing smaller. "Doesn't look like they plan to."

"Hopefully not."

Suddenly Sean let out a raw curse.

She looked over at him. "What?"

He spun her away by her shoulders. "Swim toward shore as fast as you can, and splash your feet as much as possible. Don't look back."

At the grim and dismal look on his face she felt the tears well up anew. "Sean, what is it? What's wrong?"

"Swear to me you won't look back, no matter what." She nodded, tears cresting her lashes. "Good girl. Now go. *Go!*"

She started swimming. Behind her she heard him splash off in the opposite direction. She had to know what was going on. She had to. She turned her head to look. The blood froze in her veins.

A shark fin of a very different shape than last time was cutting through the water. Heading straight for Sean.

And bearing down a hundred yards behind it was the big bay cruiser.

Chapter 17

He was so screwed.

Sean swam like a fiend, trying to get as far away from Zoë as possible before the shark hit him. This time it wasn't a harmless sand tiger. It was a real tiger. The all-too-often lethal variety. Damn that cut! He should have been more careful slicing the tape from his wrists. He should have thought. Fresh blood attracted sharks like picnics attracted ants. Army ants. With big, huge teeth that—

Goddamn it! He was *not* going to die! Not after surviving this long.

He pulled his knife, prepared to go down fighting like hell, and whipped around in the water. Just in time to see the big cruiser cut the shark off from him like a giant dog herding a sheep. He heard the rebel whoop of someone on deck as they gave chase.

What the hell was going on? Why on earth would a pack of drug smugglers who'd just tried to blow him up save his life? If being eaten by a shark wasn't good enough, he could only imagine the forms of torture they had in mind.

Except he'd rather not.

The vessel circled around and again Sean started swimming like hell. Futile, of course. No one could outswim a boat. But he could lead them farther away from Zoë. Give her a fighting chance. Hopefully she'd followed his orders. He couldn't stop to check her position, but prayed she'd made it at least into the bay so someone might see her.

Moments later the big boat glided up alongside him. Okay, so this was it. He just hoped it was quick.

"Hey! Why you swimmin' so dang fast, boy?" a familiar voice boomed from the deck.

Sean halted, coughing in surprise and spitting saltwater. He squinted up. *Tony.* Leaning against the rail, grinning and holding a submachine gun pointed in the air like some kind of cowboy gone terribly wrong. He was wearing a baseball cap and a navy blue windbreaker.

What the…

"Glad to see you made it, buddy! Heard the explosion." Tony turned and yelled at someone Sean couldn't see, "Throw the man down the ladder, will ya?"

That's when Sean noticed the markings on the boat. And the back of Tony's windbreaker. There, spelled out in big, gold letters, was the answer to his prayers. Some of them, anyway.

Good ol' Tony was an agent for the DEA.

* * *

Zoë couldn't stop shaking. Even though she and Sean had been rescued and were now wrapped in big fluffy towels, drinking hot coffee and eating Aruna's famous macadamia-nut waffles in the Indigo's sunny kitchen with Tony and the rest of the DEA crew, she still couldn't stop the trembling in her hands as she held her mug.

All she'd ever wanted was a life of excitement and adventure. Well, she'd gotten that, all right. And was definitely rethinking the whole concept. Quiet and boring was sounding pretty good about now.

Sean put a reassuring hand on her knee under the table.

"Please explain to me how a DEA vessel just happened to be lurking outside Indigo Bay ready to rescue us?" he asked Tony. "Not that I'm complaining, mind you," he added with a wry smile.

The good ol' boy grinned back. "What, y'all didn't notice me tailing you for the past few days? I was sure you'd catch on."

Sean took a sip from his mug. "Yeah, we noticed you kept on turning up everywhere. Never saw that big boat, though."

"Why would you be tailing us?" Zoë asked in surprise. She'd just thought he was a regular tourist hitting all the sights on Taveuni.

Tony scarfed down another bite of waffle. "Few weeks ago we busted a suspected drug ring up on Rotuma Island. Couldn't make the charges stick, but we pieced together the gist of their operation, which involved passing product to several middlemen who'd in turn sell it to dealers all over the region. We've been chasing down suspects ever since."

"The Blantons," Zoë said. Tony nodded. So that's what the couple had been up to. Drug-running.

"We got word of the murders down here and the argument about the missing yacht," Tony continued. "Figured it could be gang infighting, or a rival outfit trying to take over, or something like that."

Zoë exchanged a glance with Sean and gave him a wobbly smile. Close to what they'd thought, as well. Maybe they weren't so bad at this after all.

Tony looked at him, too. "When you were arrested for the murders, we thought for sure you were involved. The rival maybe, or part of the gang," Tony said, helping himself to another waffle. "So we started following you around, and I've got to say, your actions were a tad suspicious there, buddy."

Zoë's mouth dropped open. "But he told you he was looking for his yacht!"

Tony's brow hiked. "Exactly."

Sean chuckled under a wince. "What convinced you I was innocent?"

"When we learned about the similar killings on American Samoa we started having serious doubts about the killings, and therefore you. But your yacht still seemed to be connected. Then it blew up with y'all on it, and we arrested the real scumbags running from the scene with the money and enough drugs to keep the city of Atlanta high for a year. Kind of a clincher." He made a noise of disgust. "Ruthless, greedy bastards. Wish I could feed *them* to the sharks."

"Me, too," Zoë murmured. She slipped her hand into Sean's. She'd never been so terrified in her life as when she'd seen that shark heading straight for him.

Yeah, she'd been scared out of her mind when she'd thought they were both about to die. But to survive only to watch Sean being torn limb from limb by a shark, that would have been far, far worse.

Seeing that DEA boat churning to his rescue, flags flying and hull gleaming in the morning sun, had been like witnessing an arc sent down from heaven—once she'd realized it wasn't the drug dealers returning to finish the job.

"Thank you for saving him," she said, looking at the five agents' smiling faces one by one. "For saving us."

"Our pleasure, ma'am," Tony assured her.

As the men continued to talk, she closed her eyes and leaned her head against Sean's shoulder.

It was good to be alive.

But as she inhaled the comforting scent of him, she couldn't help but wonder. What would tomorrow bring?

"Phone's for you, Miss Zoë."

Zoë looked up from her chair on the verandah where she was busy filling out the final paperwork for her evaluation of the Indigo Inn. She had wanted to finish so she could e-mail it to the Secret Traveler before tomorrow's deadline.

Tomorrow. The day she was supposed to leave for her next assignment.

The morning and most of the afternoon had been crazy. She and Sean had given their individual statements to the DEA and the local police—thankfully they had not sent Inspector Sanjit. They'd talked to reporters who had descended, and answered the excited questions of the inn's guests. And eaten the endless meals and snacks Aruna had prepared in an endless succession for the crowd. When Zoë had gone outside to do her paperwork, Sean was on the phone with the FBI special agent who'd just arrived in Fiji from the States, a man named Griffin Malone, who according to Tony's contacts, was a criminal profiler of some sort.

She and Sean had not been alone together all day. Yet all she really wanted was have him take her to bed, wrap his arms around her and hold her. Just hold her.

But he was so busy, it almost felt like he was trying to avoid her.

"Miss Zoë? Are you all right?"

She snapped out of her thoughts and nodded with a smile. "Yes, thank you, Aruna. Phone for me? Do you know who it is?"

Maybe it was one of her friends and fellow Secret Travelers, Alicia or Madeline, checking up on her. It seemed like a year had gone by since they'd dropped her and her suitcases off on the Indigo's dock. So much had happened since then. Enough to last a lifetime…

"It is a man. Very businesslike."

Her boss? Maybe Mr. Cameron wanted the results of her report verbally. He was Sean's good friend, so he'd probably be interested in hearing her comments as soon as possible.

She went into a small study off the great room where the phone was kept. "Hello?"

"Zoë, it's Matt Cameron. Heard you had some excitement. How are you doing?"

"It was a little hairy there for a while, but I'm fine. Sean, too."

"Excellent. Wouldn't want to lose either of you. Now. About your evaluation. How'd my old frat bro do with that wreck of an inn? Better than one star this time?"

"Yes, indeed. I'd give it a solid five stars," she said, and proceeded to give him a rundown of the improvements and amenities. He seemed pleased and impressed.

"The guy always was an obsessive workaholic. Once he got something in his mind he didn't stop until he had it bagged. Made him a very rich man once and probably will again. Of course, it also cost him his marriage."

"Yeah," she said neutrally. The description reminded her of her father, not of Sean. But then, she hadn't really known Sean under normal circumstances. "Listen, Matt. I have a question for you."

"Shoot."

She fingered the sapphire pendant hanging around her neck. "Do you have any evaluators who don't live in Chicago? Or even the States?"

"Sure, we have two or three who live overseas. Why?"

"Oh, I was toying with the idea of moving here."

"After being there a *week*? Why?" His voice registered surprise. "Is the place *that* nice?"

"Um…"

"Ah." His tone changed to a knowing one. "I get it. He seduced you, didn't he?"

"I wouldn't exactly call it—"

"I should have known." Matt's dry remark didn't exactly give off disapproval, more like recognition.

"Our relationship didn't affect my rating, honestly. I've been scrupulously—"

"I believe you. But Zoë, listen to me. Sean Guthrie is one of my best friends. I love him dearly and he's got every reason to be the way he is. But trust me, I'd never let my sister near the man. He's left a string of broken hearts extending halfway around the world."

"He's changed, Matt."

"That's what they all thought. Right up until he gave them their walking papers."

"That's not fair," she protested, her heart squeezing. Or could he be right? He had known Sean a lot longer than she had.

"I'd hate to see you get hurt, Zoë. You've done good work for me and have a bright future here at the Secret Traveler. But I can't promote you to the A-team without more evidence you can handle the expanded responsibility. There's a big difference between overseas luxury resorts and the local Motel Nine in Bismarck."

She pushed out a breath. "I understand."

He must have read her disappointment. Possibly her disbelief in his opinion of Sean. "Finish your assignment in Fiji, Zoë. Two more resorts, different islands, away from Sean. Look at it as a test. If he lets you go, if he doesn't call, you have your answer."

She was still thinking about her boss's advice when they hung up a few minutes later.

Could he possibly be right about Sean? In her heart it felt wrong, but… All the evidence in her head pointed to Matt being right. Sean had never once mentioned anything long-term. Well, other than a shotgun wedding, offered under duress.

And what if she really was pregnant? Which she wasn't. Wrong time of month, she told herself again. Not a factor.

But even if she were, she would *not* want that to be the reason Sean asked her to stay. God knew, she loved him. But she deserved better than that old clichéd scenario. She wanted any relationship they might have to be because of herself. Because he loved *her*.

Was she deluding herself? About the whole thing? Possibly.

Maybe it was just the rush of having a new lover that made him treat her with such loving warmth. Maybe it was the same reason that made him seem so… perfect…to her.

God, this was complicated.

She should take Matt's advice. Go on to her next assignment. See what happened.

Yes. That's what she'd do. Then, one way or the other, she'd have her answer once and for all.

She just prayed it was the right one.

Something was wrong. Sean could feel it.

He and Zoë had always exchanged glances throughout the day, regardless of their moods. Warm, angry, tempting, mischievous, come-here-I-want-you. Whatever the variety, they'd never been able to keep their eyes off each other.

But now her eyes wouldn't even meet his.

What was going on?

"Aruna said you got a phone call earlier," Sean said, putting his arm around her, wanting to break the silence that shrouded them.

The DEA guys had left after an early supper. He and Zoë had finally managed to slip free of the Indigo and his guests, and were now sitting on the boathouse verandah sipping drinks and watching the sunset.

"From Matt Cameron," she replied. "He wanted my report on the inn."

"And what did you tell him?" he asked, stifling a yawn. For someone who'd had all his eggs in that particular basket only a week ago, he'd grown amazingly indifferent about the results. And the fact that Tony had told him there might be some reward money coming from the drug bust, and the insurance company was being incredibly generous about the *Hasty*, had nothing to do with it.

He'd simply realized there were more important things in life than meeting financial goals.

"The truth," she answered, darting him a quick look, then looking away just as quickly. "The Indigo deserves a five-star rating. No one could dispute that who'd seen what you've done with the place. Regardless of the unusual activities this week, or our…involvement."

Involvement.

Not relationship. Not affair. Not love.

Involvement.

Yep. Something was wrong.

"What else did he say?" he asked, beginning to suspect the source of her sudden change.

After a pause, she said, "He said he won't promote me to the international team without more evaluations under my belt. If I want to keep my job I have to do my other two assignments on Fiji."

Okay. "I guess I can understand that." Not that he liked it. "You told him about us?"

She took a sip of her drink. "Didn't have to. He guessed."

He grimaced. "My sordid past bites me in the butt."

She chuckled, but it sounded emptier than her usual teasing laugh. Hollow.

He tightened his arm and tipped up her face, wondering what the hell his good friend had said to her. "You know I'm a changed man, right?"

She smiled reflectively. "One can only hope."

He could give her more than hope. He could show her how serious he was about her. And finally tell her. He brushed her lips with his. "The sun's down. Let's go to bed."

She came willingly, letting him take off her clothes and sliding into his bed and his arms with a soft sigh and an adoring, if fragile, smile.

Their warm, naked bodies made long, slow love to each other. It had never been so good with another woman. Never felt so right before. Zoë was the only one who'd ever been able to pull him out of his work-centered emotional desert.

God, he never wanted to let her go. He *would* never let her go.

Except she *had* to go. To finish her assignments. He understood she didn't want to lose her job. He'd be a jerk to ask it of her.

Two weeks. He could deal with that. Then he'd call Matt Cameron and tell him to promote her or she was history. She wasn't ever going back to Chicago.

Okay, so he was a jerk. She was *his*. She belonged with him.

"What are you thinking?" she whispered as he lay

on top of her, their bodies slick with sweat and replete with satisfaction.

"How much I want you to stay here with me."

She gazed up at him, her eyes solemn. She laid her hand against his cheek and caressed his bottom lip with her thumb. "I can't."

"You won't."

"We've talked about this. I—"

"Damn it, Zoë, I *love* you. I want you with me!"

The words blurted out, petulant and angry, before he could stop himself and make them sound gentle and devoted, as they should be spoken.

She froze. Her lips parted and she stared wide-eyed at him for endless seconds. She swallowed heavily, then whispered so low he barely heard it, "I love you, too, Sean." His heart leapt with gladness. Until she said, "But I still have to go."

Chapter 18

"We'll see," Sean said, and covered Zoë's mouth in a drowning kiss.

She didn't dare think too hard about his words. She wanted so badly for him to stop her from boarding that plane tomorrow, to insist she stay with him. To declare his undying love and ask her hand in marriage. But that was wishful thinking. At least the last part was.

Get real. They'd only known each other a week. Just because she was being a silly, lovesick fool didn't mean he was. Sean didn't seem the foolish type. The words were sweet nectar to her heart. But she didn't think he really meant them. It was the circumstances, the emotional chaos they'd been through today, that had compelled the words from his mouth. That, and their constant, incredible lovemaking. That would blind anyone to reality.

But, oh, he did make love like a god! So when he pulled out a pair of handcuffs and bound her wrists to an upright on his ornate bamboo headboard, she didn't protest. He made love to every inch of her body, bringing her to climax once, twice, three times, with his sensual lips and his talented fingers and tongue. He knew exactly where to lick and probe her, just how hard to pinch and spank her, and the kinds of hot, wet kisses that turned her quivering insides to molten lava.

And when he'd explored every exposed and hidden part of her for hours it seemed, he covered her trembling body with his powerful frame and thrust into her with his thick, hard length, and made her come all over again just from the look in his dark, storm-blue eyes.

He uncuffed her wrists and laced his fingers with hers, pumping mercilessly until every last sensation was wrung from her, then he stiffened and came with a roar of completion, a male cry of triumph and total possession.

She felt thoroughly, utterly taken. And thoroughly, utterly shaken.

Oh, lord, what would she do when he let her go?

How could she ever make love to another man after experiencing such incredible heights with this one? How could she ever fall in love again after being so much in love with Sean Guthrie that it made her dizzy?

Rolling off, he held her close, and with a sigh she curled into his chest, seeking the warmth and solid comfort of his presence.

For as long as it lasted.

* * *

When Sean awoke, Zoë was gone from his bed.

"Baby?" he called, thinking she might be out in the kitchen.

No answer.

He let out a growl. So she thought she could get away from him by sneaking out. Had she learned nothing about him yet?

He padded naked into the bathroom and while he was taking care of business, he happened to glance down at the wastebasket. There was a tampon wrapper in it.

He squeezed his eyes shut. Disappointment welled over him. So much for *that* reason to stay. Well, she'd warned him. And to be truly honest, he wasn't sure he'd been ready for that step anyway. Not yet. But in a few years…

Wandering out to the window, he pulled in a deep breath and gazed out over Indigo Bay. The sea plane scheduled to pick Zoë up was still anchored, bobbing in the surf awaiting its passenger. Her two suitcases were sitting primly on the dock next to the Indigo's dinghy. No one was in sight.

Not surprising. The pilot nearly always had breakfast at the inn on these puddle-jump runs. And if Sean knew Zoë, she'd be up there saying goodbye to Aruna and the others she'd become friends with.

Was she planning to come back to his bed and tell him goodbye, as well? Or did she just intend to fly off, leaving him without a word?

It didn't matter. Either way, he wouldn't be here. He had things to do, somewhere to be.

He'd deal with Miss Zoë Conrad when the proper time came.

In the meantime, he'd better hurry and get dressed.

His plans didn't stop just because one stubborn woman decided her job was more important than loving him.

Zoë took a deep, fortifying breath before she opened the door to Sean's bedroom. She hoped he wouldn't make a scene, yet prayed with all her heart he would. That he'd give her a sign he cared as much for her as she cared for him. Showed her that his declaration of love last night wasn't merely the great sex talking.

She pushed down the handle and swung open the door.

The spicy fragrance of his cologne wafted over her, along with the musky scent of their lovemaking, overwhelming her with longing. The bright morning sun shone its rays through the window, picking up a golden glitter of dust particles in the air, as though someone had disturbed an object long left untouched. But the bed was empty. The room was empty.

"Sean?" she called, wandering through the small confines of the boathouse. He wasn't there.

"Okay," she murmured, her heart growing heavier by the second. He must have known where she was, and that she would come back to say goodbye. He'd chosen not to stop her from leaving the island; had chosen not even to see her before she left.

She let out the painful breath she'd been holding. "Guess I have my answer, then." Great sex it was.

She would not break down. She'd be fine.

Eventually.

Straightening her spine, she walked down the stairs to the dock and signaled the pilot, who was talking to the marina attendant, that she was ready to go.

He nodded and the three of them got into the dinghy. Determinedly holding back her tears, she took one final look backward, then turned her watery gaze toward the sea plane that would take her away from the Indigo Inn. Away from Sean. Away from the million pieces of her shattered heart.

"Grab any spot you like and be sure to buckle up," the pilot said as he helped her climb into the small cabin.

There wasn't a lot of choice. Just two tall seats facing forward on either side of the aisle, though she could see the backs of two more facing the other way, sharing a window in pairs. She tossed her purse on the farthest seat, intending to take the closest facing forward.

She turned. And saw him.

Sitting in the backward seat, looking at her like an angry wolf. She gasped.

"Sean!"

The plane roared to life with a jolt and she fell back into her seat.

"What are you doing here?" she asked breathlessly, battling not to let her tears come bursting out. From either misery or joy.

Judging by the look on his face, misery.

"You forgot to wake me up this morning."

"I, um—"

"You really expected me to let you leave like that?"

She had prayed he wouldn't. But expected? Not so much.

"I'm sorry. You looked so—" *Handsome? Sexy? Absolutely perfect?* "So peaceful lying there in bed. I hated to disturb you."

He leaned forward and fastened her seat belt in a swift motion just before the plane revved up and started to skim and scup across the waves.

He was still scowling. "Coward," he said, but there was no real heat behind the word.

"Yeah," she admitted shakily.

The roar of the engines during takeoff was too loud to hear his reply. Probably just as well.

"I could have sworn you said you loved me," he said when the noise level evened out to a steady hum. It wasn't exactly an accusation. But close.

"I do!" she blurted out. Wanting him to know that she, at least, had been sincere.

"Say it again, then. Aloud."

She swallowed heavily. It was far too late for pride. Better to be honest. "I love you, Sean. With all my heart."

His eyes bored into her. "And yet, here you are."

She looked down at her hands, clenched in her lap. Waiting… Waiting… "I was hoping…"

"What were you hoping?" he asked when she didn't continue.

"I was hoping that—" *That he'd say it back. That he'd say it like he meant it, like he had last night. Sort of.* She gave herself a mental shake. "That things could be different."

She darted a glance at him and the piercing intensity in his eyes captured hers and held them. She couldn't look away if she wanted to.

"Would this make things different enough?" He held out what looked like an old lace handkerchief tied into a small bundle. "Open it."

Her heart stuttered as she slowly reached out and let him deposit it on her palm. "What is it?"

He didn't reply, just raised a brow and nodded his head at the bundle.

Her pulse took off. Along with her imagination.

Don't hope! Don't you dare hope! It's not what you think....

With shaking fingers she plucked at the loose knot and carefully opened the handkerchief. And sucked in a breath of confused, awestruck shock. It was—

A ring. A *diamond* ring! An absolutely gorgeous ring with a large center stone surrounded by smaller ones that sparkled brilliantly in an antique gold setting.

She looked up at the man she loved with all her soul. This time she couldn't stop the tears from spilling over her lashes.

"Oh, Sean," she said on a soft sob.

He took the ring and slipped it on her finger. "Marry me, Zoë. Marry me and have my children and grow old with me."

Her heart soared on wings of joy. "Really?" she whispered, aching, yearning for it to be true. "You really mean it?"

"I love you like crazy, woman, and if you think I'll just let you walk away from me, you don't know me very well."

"Oh, Sean," she managed to choke out. "Yes! Yes,

I'll marry you!" She leaned forward and threw her arms around his neck. "I never thought… I thought…"

"Shh. I told you you're mine. I meant it."

"But what about—"

"If it's your job you're worried about, don't. I'm coming with you."

She pulled back and looked wonderingly at him. "You are?"

"I could use a vacation," he said, and winked. "I'll be your cover. We can test the amenities together." His eyebrows waggled. "Make that *under*cover."

She felt a bone-deep smile bloom all the way from her lips to her toes. "You are so bad."

"Damn straight." His answering smile was unrepentant. Just the way she liked it. "That's why you love me, baby."

Oh, yes. "From the moment I saw you lying dead in that hammock," she agreed, her entire being lighting with love for him. She was definitely the luckiest woman in the world.

"I'd say that deserves a toast."

His eyes sparkled as he reached over and opened a small fridge she hadn't noticed tucked under the window table, and pulled out two curvy glasses that glinted bright red. With a grin he offered her one.

"Bloody Mary?"

Epilogue

Zoë laughed, her heart so full of love she thought it might burst. She had never been so happy in her life.

She accepted the glass from her fiancé. Her *fiancé!*

"You brought me back to life, Zoë Conrad," he said, touching the rim of his to hers. "Here's to a hundred exciting, adventurous years together."

"I love you, Sean Guthrie. So incredibly much." They drank, then she held up her hand and once more gazed at her gorgeous ring. "It's so beautiful," she whispered. "I'm so happy."

Static from the overhead speaker buzzed through the cabin. "I take it congratulations are in order," the pilot said into his microphone, turning around with a big grin on his face. He gave Sean a thumbs-up. "Way to go, dude."

"Thanks, man," Sean said, lifting his glass in a salute.

"Hope you won't be honeymooning in Fiji," the pilot continued cheerfully.

"Why not?" Zoë asked, gazing besottedly at her man. *Her* man!

"Check out the paper," the pilot said.

Brow raised, Sean plucked the newspaper from a pouch of reading material on the wall behind him. He flipped it open. And let out a surprised curse. Then turned it toward her.

She stared in horror at the huge bold headline.

Sex-on-the-Beach Killer Strikes Fiji Again!
Two Die on the Big Island

Next to the article was a photo of the person who had discovered the bodies. Her eyes widened in dismay.

"My God. That's Alicia!"

* * * * *

Dear Reader,

Wow, is there anything better than a warm beach, a hot man and a cold drink? Toss in a dead body and in my book you've got the perfect day. (Fictional, that is!)

I recently had the opportunity to visit Fiji, the setting for *Killer Temptation,* and simply fell in love with the islands and the people. I couldn't wait to set a book there! Imagine how thrilled I was when my editor called and asked me to launch this new Silhouette Romantic Suspense summer sizzler series featuring— you got it—sex on an exotic beach! How great was that?

I really hope you enjoyed book 1. And be sure to break out the sunglasses, grab a frozen margarita (or a Bloody Mary!) and settle in for more scorching-hot summer reads with books 2 and 3 of SEDUCTION SUMMER, coming in July and August.

Until then, please check out my Web site, www.NinaBruhns.com, and drop me a line!

Good (hot!) reading!

Nina

The editors at Harlequin Blaze have never been afraid to push the limits—tempting readers with the forbidden, whetting their appetites with a wide variety of story lines. But now we're breaking the final barrier—the time barrier.

In July, watch for BOUND TO PLEASE by fan favorite Hope Tarr, Harlequin Blaze's first ever historical romance—a story that's truly Blaze-worthy in every sense.

Here's a sneak peek…

BRIANNA stretched out beside Ewan, languid as a cat, and promptly fell asleep. Midday sunshine streamed into the chamber, bathing her lovely, long-limbed body in golden light, the sea-scented breeze wafting inside to dry the damp red-gold tendrils curling about her flushed face. Propping himself up on one elbow, Ewan slid his gaze over her. She looked beautiful and whole, satisfied and sated, and altogether happier than he had so far seen her. A slight smile curved her beautiful lips as though she must be in the midst of a lovely dream. She'd molded her lush, lovely body to his and laid her head in the curve of his shoulder and settled in to sleep beside him. For the longest while he lay there turned toward her, content to watch her sleep, at near perfect peace.

Not wholly perfect, for she had yet to answer his marriage proposal. Still, she wanted to make a baby with him, and Ewan no longer viewed her plan as the travesty he once had. He wanted children—sons to carry on after him, though a bonny little daughter with flame-colored hair would be nice, too. But he also wanted more than to simply plant his seed and be on his way. He wanted to lie beside Brianna night upon night as she increased, rub soothing unguents into the swell of her belly, knead the ache from her back and make slow, gentle love to her. He wanted to hold his newly born child in his arms and look down into Brianna's tired but radiant face and blot the perspiration from her brow and be a husband to her in every way.

He gave her a gentle nudge. "Brie?"

"Hmm?"

She rolled onto her side and he captured her against his chest. One arm wrapped about her waist, he bent to her ear and asked, "Do you think we might have just made a baby?"

Her eyes remained closed, but he felt her tense against him. "I don't know. We'll have to wait and see."

He stroked his hand over the flat plane of her belly. "You're so small and tight it's hard to imagine you increasing."

"All women increase no matter how large or small they start out. I may not grow big as a croft, but I'll be big enough, though I have hopes I may not waddle like a duck, at least not too badly."

The reference to his fair-day teasing was not lost on him. He grinned. "Brianna MacLeod grown so large she must sit still for once in her life. I'll need the proof of my own eyes to believe it."

Despite their banter, he felt his spirits dip. Assuming they were so blessed, he wouldn't have the chance to see her thus. By then he would be long gone, restored to his clan according to the sad bargain they'd struck. He opened his mouth to ask her to marry him again and then clamped it closed, not wanting to spoil the moment, but the unspoken words weighed like a millstone on his heart.

The damnable bargain they'd struck was proving to be a devil's pact indeed.

* * * * *

Will these two star-crossed lovers find
their sexily-ever-after?
Find out in BOUND TO PLEASE by Hope Tarr,
available in July wherever Harlequin® Blaze™
books are sold.

Harlequin Blaze marks new territory with its first historical novel!

For years readers have trusted the Harlequin Blaze series to entertain them with a variety of stories—Now Blaze is breaking down the final barrier—the time barrier!

Welcome to Blaze Historicals—all the sexiness you love in a Blaze novel, all the adventure of a historical romance. It's the best of both worlds!

Don't miss the first book in this exciting new miniseries:

BOUND TO PLEASE
by Hope Tarr

New laird Brianna MacLeod knows she can't protect her land or her people without a man by her side. So what else can she do—she kidnaps one! Only, she doesn't expect to find herself the one enslaved....

Available in July wherever Harlequin books are sold.

HB79411

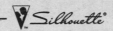

SPECIAL EDITION™

NEW YORK TIMES BESTSELLING AUTHOR

DIANA PALMER

A brand-new Long, Tall Texans novel

HEART OF STONE

Feeling unwanted and unloved, Keely returns
to Jacobsville and to Boone Sinclair, a rancher
troubled by his own past. Boone has always
seemed reserved, but now Keely discovers a
sensuality with him that quickly turns to love. Can
they each see past their own scars to let love in?

*Available September 2008
wherever you buy books.*

REQUEST YOUR FREE BOOKS!

2 FREE NOVELS PLUS 2 FREE GIFTS!

Silhouette® Romantic

SUSPENSE

Sparked by Danger, Fueled by Passion!

YES! Please send me 2 FREE Silhouette® Romantic Suspense novels and my 2 FREE gifts (gifts are worth about $10). After receiving them, if I don't wish to receive any more books, I can return the shipping statement marked "cancel." If I don't cancel, I will receive 4 brand-new novels every month and be billed just $4.24 per book in the U.S. or $4.99 per book in Canada, plus 25¢ shipping and handling per book plus applicable taxes, if any*. That's a savings of at least 15% off the cover price! I understand that accepting the 2 free books and gifts places me under no obligation to buy anything. I can always return a shipment and cancel at any time. Even if I never buy another book from Silhouette, the two free books and gifts are mine to keep forever.

240 SDN EEX6   340 SDN EEYJ

Name	(PLEASE PRINT)

Address		Apt. #

City	State/Prov.	Zip/Postal Code

Signature (if under 18, a parent or guardian must sign)

Mail to the Silhouette Reader Service:
IN U.S.A.: P.O. Box 1867, Buffalo, NY 14240-1867
IN CANADA: P.O. Box 609, Fort Erie, Ontario L2A 5X3

Not valid to current subscribers of Silhouette Romantic Suspense books.

Want to try two free books from another line?
Call 1-800-873-8635 or visit www.morefreebooks.com.

* Terms and prices subject to change without notice. N.Y. residents add applicable sales tax. Canadian residents will be charged applicable provincial taxes and GST. Offer not valid in Quebec. This offer is limited to one order per household. All orders subject to approval. Credit or debit balances in a customer's account(s) may be offset by any other outstanding balance owed by or to the customer. Please allow 4 to 6 weeks for delivery. Offer available while quantities last.

Your Privacy: Silhouette is committed to protecting your privacy. Our Privacy Policy is available online at www.eHarlequin.com or upon request from the Reader Service. From time to time we make our lists of customers available to reputable third parties who may have a product or service of interest to you. If you would prefer we not share your name and address, please check here. ☐

SRS08R

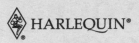

COMING NEXT MONTH

#1519 A SOLDIER'S HOMECOMING—Rachel Lee
Conard County: The Next Generation
When he learns the truth about his father, military man Ethan Parish is determined to reunite with his long-lost family in Wyoming. On his way into town, he clashes with policewoman Connie Halloran, whose captivating beauty entices him. Together, they confront the dangers inherent in family secrets.

#1520 KILLER PASSION—Sheri WhiteFeather
Seduction Summer
Racked with guilt over his wife's murder, Agent Griffin Malone tries to get his life back on track. Enter Alicia Greco, an attractive and accomplished analyst for a travel company. The two meet and find passion, which is exactly what puts them into a serial killer's sights. Will they escape the island's curse on lovers?

#1521 SNOWBOUND WITH THE BODYGUARD—Carla Cassidy
Wild West Bodyguards
Single mom Janette Black needs to protect her baby from repeated threats by the girl's father. Fleeing for their lives, she knows bodyguard Dalton West is the only man who can help. After taking them in, they brave a snowstorm and discover a sense of home. This time, can Janette trust that she's found the perfect sanctuary...and lasting love?

#1522 DUTY TO PROTECT—Beth Cornelison
Crisis counselor Ginny West is trapped in an office fire when firefighter Riley Sinclair walks into her life. A bond forms between the two, especially when he keeps saving her from a menacing client. As danger still looms, one defining moment forces the pair to reassess their combustible relationship.

SRSCNM0608